"How am I doing so far?" Gemma asked

"All right," was Robb's laconic reply.

Anger rose in her. "Is that all you can say? I was almost killed by a herd of brumbies, and all you can say is 'all right'?"

"We're not given to lavish compliments in the bush, Gemma. 'All right' is the equivalent of 'bloody marvelous.'"

"Well, you might have said so in the first place," she replied. "Lord, I wonder what you say when you *really* get excited."

Robb suddenly moved toward her, almost threateningly. "What are you doing?" Laura asked nervously.

He towered over her. "I don't say much when something excites me. What I *do* is another matter."

To her absolute astonishment, he leaned down, lifted her to her feet and captured her mouth in a sudden, totally passionate kiss. . . .

Valerie Parv had a busy and successful career as a journalist and advertising copywriter before she began writing for Harlequin in 1982. She is an enthusiastic member of several Australian writers' organizations. Her many interests include her husband, her cat and the Australian environment. Her love of the land is a distinguishing feature in many of her books for Harlequin. She has recently written a colorful study in a nonfiction book titled *The Changing Face of Australia*. Her home is in New South Wales.

Books by Valerie Parv

Snowy River Man
Valerie Parv

Harlequin Books

TORONTO • NEW YORK • LONDON
AMSTERDAM • PARIS • SYDNEY • HAMBURG
STOCKHOLM • ATHENS • TOKYO • MILAN

Original hardcover edition published in 1987
by Mills & Boon Limited

ISBN 0-373-02934-9

Harlequin Romance first edition September 1988

CHAPTER ONE

THE sign above the hotel said 'Servicing the High Country for over a hundred years'. Alongside it was a more modern sign promising 'The best five icy cold beers in Omeo'.

The noise from within indicated the pub was open, Gemma Tate thought with relief as she pushed open the door marked 'Public Bar'. It was late on a Saturday and everything else in the Victorian cattle town was closed.

As she stood in the opening, surveying the crowded bar, the noise began to die down and the closely packed men holding glasses of beer looked curiously her way.

'Ladies' lounge is through there, love,' a florid man behind the bar told her, indicating the way with a jerk of his head.

She smiled warmly. 'I don't want to drink, thanks. I was hoping for some advice.'

'You're still not supposed to be in here,' the barman persisted, aware that her presence was provoking a groundswell of disapproval from his customers.

Ignoring the interested looks she was getting, Gemma walked up to the bar. As a journalist, she had ventured into worse places and she knew the men meant no real harm. Most of them were probably married with children and would run a mile if she acknowledged their suggestions.

She could hardly help attracting their attention. Even casually dressed in jeans, Jag shirt and boots, there was no disguising her undeniably feminine curves. And her silky blonde hair swung around her shoulders, adding to the effect.

The barman took her arm. 'We can talk in the lounge, love.'

'It's all right. I'm fine here.'

Short of removing her bodily, the barman had to be content, but he was far from comfortable about her invasion of this strictly male territory. Hadn't he heard of the Equal Opportunities Act?

She decided to put the poor man out of his misery. 'I'm Gemma Tate from *Outback* magazine,' she explained, 'I'm doing a story about the High Country and I need a guide to take me to some remote areas.'

'Only one man for the job,' mumbled the barman. 'Robb Wetherill. He runs a safari business just outside town—fishing, bushwalking, ski touring in winter, you know.'

She cocked her head thoughtfully, aware that there was now almost total silence around the crowded bar. Wetherill. No, he wouldn't do at all. 'Can you recommend someone else?' she asked tensely.

The barman smiled apologetically. 'I'm sorry. Robb's the only one working around here this season. Besides, he's the best there is.' He looked around the bar and several customers murmured agreement.

It looked as though she had no choice. In any case there was no reason why Robb Wetherill should recognise her, or attach any importance to her present surname. 'Very well,' she sighed. 'Where do I find Mr Wetherill?'

Relieved to be seeing her on her way, the barman gave driving directions to the Wetherill house, which he said she would find a few miles out of the town off the main Omeo Road.

Thanking him, she turned to leave and immediately heard the chatter start up again. She smiled to herself as she walked back to her car. These men were a chauvinistic lot. She wondered whether Mr Robb Wetherill would be the same.

Following the barman's directions, she drove along the macadam, then on to a dirt road into the bush, through groves of towering eucalypt trees. The going became steeper.

In protest at the demands made upon it, her car developed a worrying sluggishness. She crossed her fingers. A breakdown here, miles from anywhere, would be disastrous.

When she was just about to give up and head back to Omeo, a house appeared in a clearing.

It was an A-framed cottage built of mud bricks and hardwood, and rimmed by a veranda. Since it was the only building around, it had to belong to the man she sought. She responded to its welcoming appearance immediately. With such a home, Mr Wetherill couldn't be too much of an ogre.

Her boots clip-clopped on the tallow-wood veranda and she listened for answering footsteps from inside. There were none. Nor was there any response to her knock on the flyscreen door.

Mr Wetherill must be out. But judging by the

invitingly open front door beyond the screen, he couldn't be far. Exhausted after her long drive, she debated whether or not to wait inside, then decided he was unlikely to mind. She was about to become a client, after all.

The door opened into a spacious living-room lined with pine. Above her, an A-frame ceiling soared to a loft level. The preponderence of timber and a collection of art-deco-style rugs and cushions scattered around gave the room a definitely masculine air. She wondered if Mr Wetherill lived here alone.

'Anyone home?' she called and her voice echoed hollowly up to the rafters.

When there was no answer, she moved further inside and noticed a desk, its top almost obscured by papers. In the middle of the chaos stood a telephone linked to a modern answering machine.

She moved to it and flicked a switch. As she had hoped, a male voice echoed through the room.

'G'day. This is Robb Wetherill of Adventure Safaris. I've been called away on urgent business but I'll be glad to call you back in an hour. Please leave your name and telephone number after you hear the beep sound.'

Gemma turned the machine off as soon as she heard the piercing tone, not wanting to eavesdrop on any of Mr Wetherill's messages.

So he was due back fairly soon. Even if he had only just left, she had a maximum of an hour to wait for his return.

She curled up on a comfortable upholstered couch. Judging from the voice, her prospective guide was youngish, around thirty she would guess. For some reason she thought he sounded tall. There was a lot of authority in that voice, as if he was accustomed to giving orders. He sounded like a man to be reckoned with.

A shiver ran down her spine. He couldn't be the original Mr Wetherill her mother had told her about. That would make him around sixty, and in any case she was sure that man's first name had been Mick. So Robb must be a son, or relative, of the other Mr Wetherill.

'Stop worrying,' she told herself firmly. The time to chicken out was before she persuaded her editor to give her this assignment, not now she had driven all the way from Canberra to the High Plains of Victoria.

What was she worried about anyway? She had never met any of the Wetherills and the surname she used now should not evoke any response from him.

All the same, she felt tense and nervous. What if Robb did somehow connect her with her family? He wouldn't want to help her then. And she had to find out the truth one way or the other.

The problem nagged at her until she forced herself to settle back on the couch and close her eyes, willing herself to relax.

She was more successful than she had intended, because she soon drifted off to sleep, exhausted by the drive and the strain of coming here.

'Hello, Sleeping Beauty.'

She opened her eyes to find someone bending over her and she felt a jolt almost of recognition. But it was more the recognition of woman to man than anything else.

Even from this angle, she was aware of the man's

impressive six feet in height and the width of his shoulders which blocked out the daylight. He was clad in grey moleskins, a checked shirt and suede cartridge jacket, and he looked every inch the hunter.

Squirming to sit up, she knew just how a rabbit felt, caught in a shooter's spotlight. She mustered her voice with an effort. 'Hello. You must be Robb Wetherill.'

Solemnly, he shook the hand she extended. 'Delighted, Miss . . .?'

'Tate,' she supplied with the slightest hint of hesitation. 'I'm a writer with *Outback* magazine.'

He regarded her with interest. 'You're G D Tate.'

She coloured with pleasure at the recognition in his voice. 'You've read some of my articles?'

'Quite a few. But I didn't expect to find their author asleep in my living-room.'

'I'm sorry about that. But it was a long drive. The door was open, and I didn't think you'd mind if I waited inside. I didn't intend to fall asleep.'

'Think nothing of it,' he said smoothly, 'Now you're awake, what can I do for you?'

This was the tricky part. 'I'm told you're the best guide in the High Country. I'm here on assignment and I'd like to retain your services.'

She had intended to come right out and say what the assignment was, but she found it was harder than she had anticipated. He might not be interested anyway, she thought, half hoping he would turn her down and save her the effort of explaining.

But his eyes lighted with interest. 'Sounds good. I don't know about the best guide in the area, though.'

'That's what they told me at the hotel in Omeo.'

'I must buy the barman a drink for that,' he laughed. She nodded. 'Is he a friend of yours?'

'In a town of only a few hundred people, everybody's a friend of mine,' he confirmed. Then he straightened. 'I was about to make myself some dinner. Would you like to join me while we talk about your assignment?'

Temptation tugged at her but she resisted it. Spending time alone with him at his home was not part of her plans. Resolutely, she checked her watch. 'It's tempting, but it's later than I thought. I'll leave you to your dinner and come back to talk business tomorrow.'

Coward, she told herself as she took her leave. She was just putting off the need to explain what she wanted. It wasn't that she was afraid of the indomitable Mr Wetherill, surely?

'Tomorrow, then.' He watched from the doorway as she climbed into her car with unseemly haste. She would be glad to escape from his disturbing scrutiny.

But her car betrayed her. Good old reliable, veteran of many assignments in out-of-the-way places, it chose that moment to die on her. No amount of cursing or coaxing would start it again.

After a thorough inspection of the engine, even Robb Wetherill pronounced himself beaten. 'It must be the electrical system. I'll phone the mechanic in Omeo and get him to come up and look at it.'

'Oh, no,' she wailed. 'Can you give me a lift to town so I can see him, and arrange a room for the night?'

His smile was curiously devoid of regret. 'I'm afraid

not. I lent my car to Doc Barnes until Friday.'

She smiled wanly. 'What am I going to do?'

'There's a spare room here you can use.'

'Oh, I couldn't impose on you. Your wife would be horrified.'

There was a definite gleam in his eyes as he said, 'In the first place, there's no Mrs Wetherill to object, and in the second, you wouldn't be imposing. If we're to spend some time together under the stars, what's the difference if we share my roof for the first night?'

Put like that, it didn't sound so disturbing, she had to admit. All the same, she resisted the idea. It wasn't that she was afraid of Robb Wetherill. Quite the opposite, in fact. There was a lot about him which inspired her confidence. But there was a formidable air about him which put her on her guard. He looked lean and physically fit. Proud and dangerous were the adjectives which came most readily to mind.

His nose looked as if it couldn't decide whether to go east or west. Maybe he had broken it in a skiing accident some time. His skin was burned dark by exposure to sun and snow, and outdoorsy furrows creased the skin around his eyes. They were compelling, too, light-coloured and flecked with gold like a tiger's. But it was his mouth which arrested her gaze. It was narrow and almost arrogant, except when he smiled, then he looked devastatingly attractive.

He was a Wetherill, she reminded herself. Sharing a house with him, even for one night, she might betray who she really was, then she would have no chance of enlisting his help. But with no means of getting back to town, what else could she do? 'I don't know,' she said diffidently.

'I don't bite, I promise,' he affirmed. He handed her the telephone handset. 'Here, call anyone you like and they'll vouch for how trustworthy I am.'

She smiled unvoluntarily. 'I have no doubt they would. But then I don't know if I can trust them either.'

'Then you'll just have to accept my word that you'll be safe here until I can get someone to tow your car back to Omeo.'

'Safe' was hardly a word she would use in connection with a man like Robb Wetherill, she thought. But she had very little choice, so she nodded agreement. 'Very well, I'll stay, and thank you for the invitation.'

'My pleasure.' He held up a metal ring from which swung some glistening rainbow trout. 'You do like fish, I take it?'

'So that was the urgent business you were called away to attend,' she murmured, her tone amused.

His gaze flickered to the answering machine. 'Ah yes, the intrepid journalist has discovered my guilty secret. All right, I confess, I went fishing. But it was urgent. There was nothing in the refrigerator for dinner.'

In spite of the hazards, she found herself liking him more and more. 'In that case, you did the right thing,' she agreed solemnly, unable to keep the humour out of her voice.

His answering smile engulfed her. She felt transfixed by its intensity and she froze, unable to break free.

Finally, he looked away. 'You'd better get your luggage from your car, Miss Gemma Tate,' he said in a voice which was tight, not at all like his bantering tone of a moment before.

'Please call me Gemma,' she said a little breathlessly, wondering what he had seen in her to make his voice so husky.

He busied himself placing the fish on the kitchen counter. 'Very well, Gemma. And I'm Robb.'

As she lifted her case out of the back seat of her car, she resisted an urge to give the tyres a mighty kick.

Of all times for the car to play up, why did it have to be now when she was stranded miles from anywhere? She could have insisted on borrowing one of the horses she could see roaming in a paddock near the house, but she didn't want to sound over-eager to get away from Robb, for fear of arousing his suspicions.

With a sigh of resignation, she carried the case back inside. She was stuck here, so she would just have to watch her step. If she was careful, there was no reason for Robb to suspect that she was more than a reporter on assignment, or that her interest in this particular story was intensely personal.

Inside, the aroma of frying trout greeted her and she sniffed appreciatively. 'Mmm, smells good.'

He grinned back. 'There's nothing like freshly caught trout gently pan-fried in butter.' His eyes roved over her trim waist and the curve of her hips. 'You don't object to the butter, I take it?'

The implied compliment made her feel uncomfortable. The last thing she needed was for Robb Wetherill to start developing an interest in her. 'No, I don't,' she said shortly, turning away. 'Where shall I put my things?'

He adjusted the heat under the frying pan then opened a door off the living-room. 'You should be comfortable in here. Dinner will be in ten minutes.'

'Comfortable' was an understatement, she saw when she entered the room. A vast Tasmanian oak bedstead took up most of the floor space and was covered with a bright Mexican-weave bedspread. Behind it, in place of a head board, was a half-circle window looking out on to the verdant bushland.

The walls were of painted mud bricks and the ceiling was lined with rough-sawn Oregon planks, giving the room a rustic appearance which was warm and welcoming. A door opened off to one side, revealing a compact, well equipped bathroom, also timber-panelled.

Robb had said ten minutes, which gave her time to freshen up and decide how much to tell him about her assignment.

Her impromptu nap had refreshed her and a quick sponge bath completed the job. She freshened up her make-up, took a couple of deep breaths and returned to the living-room.

Robb was putting laden plates on the dining-table, and he pulled out a chair for her then took his place opposite. 'Now, Gemma Tate. Tell me what brings you to the High Plains.'

She took a mouthful of succulent trout and chewed it slowly, delaying the need to answer. When he still waited expectantly, she set her fork down. 'My editor wants me to do a story about something that happened around here five years ago. You may not have heard about it, of course but it was known as the *Drifter* disappearance.'

She knew he had heard of it, but added that part so that he wouldn't suspect how much she knew of the story.

At the mention of the name, *Drifter*, his jaw tightened and his eyes darkened ominously, blotting out the gold flecks. 'I've heard of it,' he said tightly. 'What possible interest can your magazine have in such old news?'

She leaned forward. 'Firstly, it's an unsolved mystery. Nobody knows what became of the pilot of the *Plains Drifter* because no trace of the plane has ever been found. And secondly, this year is the fifth anniversary of the disappearance, so it's a good time to recap the mystery.'

'There's no mystery about it,' Robb said flatly. 'The plane was never found because the pilot didn't want it to be found. He made off with the relief funds which were donated to our bushfire victims.'

'You don't know that!' she said with more passion than she intended. With an effort, she reined in her temper and said more calmly, 'There was never any proof that the pilot stole the money meant for the cattlemen.'

'Or that he crashed in the mountains,' Robb said, his voice surly.

'Exactly. That's why I . . . why my magazine wants to conduct a new investigation. We're hoping that you can guide us to the High Plains area where the plane most likely went down. If we find it with the money still on board, the mystery will be solved and the pilot will be exonerated.'

'*If* you find it. Do you realise how many people have tried without success in the last five years—and not always with the best motives, either?'

'I understand,' she went on. 'I ... looked up the morgue files on the event before I left Canberra. The air search mounted for the plane was one of the biggest ever conducted in this country.'

'So what makes you think you can do better?'

Because she had more reason than anyone to find the plane. Since she couldn't tell Robb that, she said instead, 'I believe the attempt has more chance of success from the ground. There's little hope of spotting anything from the air, don't you agree?'

Reluctantly, Robb nodded. 'But there have been ground-based expeditions and none of them have found anything.'

'I know, and I may not find anything either, but I still want to try.'

He regarded her with grudging respect. 'I can't fault your courage, Gemma Tate. But it's a fool's errand. This is the most inaccessible country in Australia. You haven't a prayer of finding anything.'

'You sound as if you don't want me to try. Is there any reason you wouldn't want the plane to be found?'

His eyes blazed, the flecks standing out as tongues of flame against the darkness of his skin. 'Yes, there's a damned good reason,' he snapped. 'My father was one of the cattlemen that pilot swindled out of the cash that might have saved his property. Because of him, we lost a property that had been in my family for three generations. Searching for the plane will only reopen those wounds.'

'Because it isn't there—or because you're afraid it is?' she asked quietly.

His gimlet eyes bored into her. 'What sort of game are you playing, Miss Tate? Everyone around here knows what happened to that money.'

'Then you shouldn't be afraid to help me confirm it.'

'I'm not afraid, damn it. I just don't see the point of setting out on some wild-goose chase that could get you killed.'

'Let me worry about that,' she said, suppressing a shiver. 'I'm very fit, and I can handle myself in rough country.'

'Not as rough as the High Plains,' he asserted. He swirled the fish around on his plate but did not eat. 'Anyway, you're only being paid to write a story. What makes you want to risk life and limb scouring these mountains, when the results can't matter to you either way?'

'I sense a good story in this,' she persisted. 'If I can solve the mystery of the *Drifter* disappearance by actually finding the plane, it will make a hell of a story.'

'And if you don't find anything?'

'Then I'll write about the people affected by the disappearance five years later.'

'We don't need that kind of publicity,' he ground out, pushing his plate away. 'Everything that could have been said about the *Drifter* disappearance was said at the time. You only have two chances of locating the plane—slim and none. I'm not the man to help you.'

'But they told me you're the best guide in the High Plains,' she said, injecting a deliberate note of disappointment into her voice.

'Maybe. I don't have to prove it to you.'

'What about to the Duncan family?' she asked, watching his expression.

'Jack Duncan should have thought of his family when he skipped off with the cattlemen's money,' he said, his tone pitiless. 'His family got the treatment they deserved. It was a good thing for everyone when they left town.'

'Was it a good thing that a grieving woman who'd already lost her husband should have to uproot her son and try to make a life for herself somewhere else?'

'I should have known where your sympathies would lie, Miss Tate,' Robb said harshly. 'A woman journalist would naturally want to write some sob-story about the poor family driven out of their home by a town's anger.'

'You said it, I didn't.'

'Well, they deserved what they got. For all we know, Jack Duncan could have rejoined them under an assumed identity, so they could all enjoy the spoils.'

'But they didn't,' she said with such assurance that Robb looked at her curiously. 'At least that's what my sources say,' she added hastily. 'Ann Duncan took her son to live with relatives in Canberra and made a poor living as a clerk in the public service. She died last year of a heart attack.'

Robb shrugged. 'So there goes your story.'

'Not quite. Other people were involved, and I can

interview them about their feelings five years after the event.'

'Go ahead. Just don't expect me to be one of them.'

'You are afraid,' she said, stunned by a sudden flash of insight. 'You're not sure yourself whether the town did the right thing in hounding the Duncan family away. You don't want the mystery solved because it would mean that your friends victimised an innocent family.'

Robb swore softly. 'You journalist types don't mind hitting below the belt, do you?'

'Then it's true? You're not convinced that Jack Duncan absconded with the Bushfire Relief funds.'

'All right, so I'm unconvinced. My father had no doubts. He led the ground search for the plane initially. When nothing was found, he was forced to sell Wyuna, our cattle property in the Snowy Valley.' His body angled forward, emphasising his point. 'But look at it from our point of view. A massive bushfire had just ripped the guts out of our land. Then we heard that a fortune had been donated to help us replace our stock and get started again. That money was our last hope. We were devastated when we heard he'd disappeared with the cash.'

'But he might have crashed. The plane could have been overlooked,' she pointed out.

He raked a hand through his hair, tousling it. 'Yes, yes, I know. The possibility has worried me ever since. When the plane wasn't found, everyone was sure it was a planned disappearance. But I had my doubts.'

'Then here's your chance to find out, one way or the other,' she urged, taking advantage of the concession.

'My magazine is willing to pay a large fee for your services in helping us look for the plane.'

'How large?' he asked.

She named a sum which brought his lips together in a soundless whistle. 'They really are keen, aren't they?'

In fact, the magazine had allocated a much smaller sum for expenses, believing, as Robb did, that nothing new would be uncovered. But she had supplemented the amount with money from her own savings. 'It will be a real scoop if we find the plane,' she reminded him. 'The reprint rights should sell all over the world.'

'And if you don't find the wreck, you'll have done your dough. What then?'

'Then we'll have done our dough, as you put it,' she responded so solemnly that his expression lightened for the first time since they sat down together.

'I'll say this for you, you've got guts and determination,' he acknowledged.

The crisis past, she smiled back. 'They're essential qualities for a journalist.'

'But you're going to need much more than that for this trip,' he cautioned her. 'Such as stamina, and endurance beyond anything you've ever had to call on before.'

'I'm sure I can handle it,' she said with more assurance than she felt. Driving up here from Omeo had given her a glimpse of the kind of country they would be traversing, and she was not at all sure she was up to it.

Robb apparently had doubts, too. 'Before we mount a full-scale expedition, I'd want to put you to the test.'

A prickle of apprehension raised the hairs on the back

of her neck. 'What kind of test?'

'A safari into the High Plains, just a couple of days of riding and bushwalking to find out if you've got what it takes.'

If that was what it took to persuade him to lead her to the plane, she was ready. 'I'll take any test you care to suggest,' she volunteered.

He regarded her keenly. 'I hope you don't regret saying that.'

Elation that she had almost achieved her aim was overlaid with apprehension. What kind of test did he have in mind?

CHAPTER TWO

NEXT morning, Gemma awoke shivering as a blast of cold air whipped across her midriff. Blearily, she opened her eyes to find Robb pulling her blankets away. She tugged them out of his hands. 'What do you think you're doing?'

'I'm not about to carry you off, if that's what's worrying you,' he said tautly. 'It's time to get up.'

She glanced over her shoulder at the half-moon window. 'It's still dark outside.'

'It's advisable to get an early start in the mountains. The weather can turn on you suddenly, so you need to make the most of the sunlit hours.'

She snorted derisively. 'Sunlight! How can you tell what sort of day it's going to be at this hour?'

He grinned at her. 'I'm the best guide in the mountains, remember?' Abruptly, his expression altered. 'You're the one who wants to prove you can handle the conditions. Keeping the same hours I do is your first test.'

'You didn't say we were going to start right away,' she grumbled.

'With both our cars unavailable, why not? But if you aren't up to it . . .' He half turned away.

'I can handle it.' She swung her legs over the side of the bed and withdrew them hastily as her bare feet encountered icy floorboards. Then she noticed steam

23

curling from a cup on her bedside table. 'You brought me coffee?'

'When we're on the trail, you'll have to make your own.'

He sounded as if he was regretting the weakness which had prompted him to bring her a cup. 'I understand, but thanks.' She sipped the hot brew thankfully. It was thick and dark with no sugar or milk. Luckily she usually drank it black, although not as strong as this. But right now, she would have drunk anything that warmed her through. The mountain cold was unbeliveable and she shivered in her thin Baby Doll pyjamas.

Noticing her tremors, he frowned. 'I hope you've brought something more sensible than those things to take with you.'

'Of course. These were meant for an air-conditioned hotel, not . . .'

'Not the eyes of a hot-blooded mountain man,' he finished. 'Don't get me wrong. I do appreciate the effect those frilly nothings create. I wouldn't be much of a man if I didn't.'

This was becoming entirely too personal. 'They weren't brought for your entertainment,' she said primly and pulled the bedspread around herself while she finished her coffee.

His gaze slid to her left hand. 'Whose amusement were they bought for? In my experience, women rarely buy such fripperies for themselves.'

She curled her bare ring finger around the coffee cup. 'Well, your experience is incomplete, because I did buy them to please myself.'

It was not entirely true. There had been a man in her life, Kenneth Shelton, an environmental specialist who also worked for *Outback* magazine. But their relationship had foundered recently, providing her with yet another compelling reason for coming here.

She had bought the revealing pyjamas when she thought she might be close to inviting Kenneth to stay overnight. When nothing came of it, she had decided to wear them to please herself.

'So there was a man involved.' Robb observed, reading her expression.

'He never saw the pyjamas,' she said dreamily, lost in her memories.

He looked at her hard for a moment. 'It was his loss.'

Before she could frame a response, he stood up. 'Breakfast will be ready in fifteen minutes.'

She had a feeling Robb meant what he said, so she shrugged out of the blanket and made for the bathroom, finishing her shower and toilette in record time.

By the time she arrived at the breakfast table, Robb was already tucking into a generous plateful of ham and eggs and fried potatoes. He lifted a metal cover off her plate as she sat down.

'What's on the agenda today?' she asked, between bites of the delicious food.

'I rang the mechanic in Omeo. He won't be able to collect your car until this afternoon. So I thought we'd leave the keys here for him and ride up into the mountains. We can find out what you're made of.'

She regarded him with sudden apprehension. 'Ride? As in horses?'

'You can ride?' he asked.

'Yes, but ... on the flat in Canberra, not in these mountains.'

'Yet you want to go looking for a plane wreck in country that no vehicle can penetrate. How did you plan to get there?'

'On foot,' she said stupidly. 'Bushwalking, I mean.'

'And so we will. But we can save time by riding in as far as we can, then backpacking from there. Don't worry,' he said helping himself to thick slabs of toast which he spread lavishly with marmalade, 'today will be the easy part. We'll ride along marked trails. Where you want to go, we'll have to blaze our own.'

Suddenly she wondered if she wasn't insane even to think of looking for the *Plains Drifter*. Maybe Robb was right. It was lost beyond recovery, or else any one of the previous expeditions would have located it.

The alternative, that it was never there at all, she didn't like to think about.

Luckily, they had so much to do preparing for the ride that she had no more time to brood on anything. It was barely nine o'clock by the time they set off along a sealed road, then on to a dirt road which led into the bush.

Robb rode ahead of her on a big bay mare, having saddled a pinto named Kael for her. She gladly let him take the lead. The so-called trail was faint and led ever upwards into the towering eucalypt forests.

Robb's house soon dropped below them as they sloshed through the Cobungra River where a couple of mountain men were fishing for trout, the only sound the whir and splash of their lures spinning out across the silvery stream. They nodded a greeting as the riders passed.

Just when Gemma began to feel as if she had been plodding uphill for a lifetime, Robb called a halt. They picnicked on chicken and salad sandwiches by the roadside, while the horses cooled off.

It was late by the time they reached the spot where Robb said they would camp for the night.

Gemma eyed the ancient grey-timbered woolshed with dismay. 'Are we going to sleep in there?'

'Yup,' came his laconic reply.

She drew a deep breath, trying not to let him see how much the prospect alarmed her. He had said this was a test and she was determined to prove she could handle any conditions he provided. If it meant sleeping in a thirty-year-old wooden building in which could live . . . anything . . . she suppressed a shudder, then so be it.

Robb showed her how to unsaddle Kael and wash him down to remove the saddle sweat and dirt of the ride, then the animals were turned loose in the remains of a nearby paddock where they rolled in the dirt and grass like foals.

'Someone must have lived up here once,' she observed, noting the sagging fences.

'These paddocks are still used for the autumn musters,' he explained. 'But in spring and summer, it's mainly bushwalkers and fishermen who come up here, and the skiers in winter, of course.'

'Of course,' she echoed. 'Your services must be in demand all year around.'

'They are. In summer, I guide tourists on fishing

and bushwalking safaris, then in winter I'm a ski instructor at the resorts, when I'm not skiing competitively.'

She could imagine him gliding down the slopes, graceful and powerful as one of the wedge-tailed eagles hovering overhead. But she noticed an edge of bitterness in his voice as he described his work. 'Don't you enjoy what you do?'

He shrugged. 'It's a living.'

'You'd rather be a cattleman,' she guessed, then could have kicked herself for introducing the very subject she should have avoided. 'Where is Wyuna from here?' she asked, now that the damage was done.

He pointed down a valley as if sighting a rifle. 'In the Snowy River valley, the other side of Omeo.'

'You miss it, don't you?' she said, moved by something in his voice as he pointed out his former family property.

'What's done is done. You can't turn back the clock.' He turned away from the view and began sorting through their saddle bags, bringing out wrapped packages of food.

She watched, fascinated, as he started a cooking-fire in a carefully cleared area, then produced a nest of cooking utensils with folding handles, in which he proceeded to cook their dinner.

Within a surprisingly short time, they were enjoying steak and onions, with mashed potatoes reconstituted from a powder. She thought she had never tasted anything so marvellous, and said so.

'It will be your turn tomorrow night,' he warned her.

Another test? 'I'm a fair cook, even over a camp fire,' she assured him.

They washed their dishes bushman-fashion, with sand and river water, then replenished the fire with some of the dead timber lying around, and sat back to watch the dancing flames. Beyond the ring of firelight, a howl chilled her blood and she sat up, staring into the darkness.

'Dingo,' Robb observed. 'Not scared, are you?'

If she was, he was the last person she would confess to. He was itching to find an excuse not to take her into the High Plains. She was damned if she would provide one.

All the same, when the blood-curdling howl came again, she moved closer to Robb. 'Are there many dingos around here?'

'Quite a few. They're mostly cross-breeds, a combination of pure-bred native dog and domestic animal gone wild,' he explained. 'They're fascinating creatures. They mate for life. But they also kill for the fun of it, which is why the farmers around here hate them so much.'

She shivered and felt his arm steal around her shoulders. 'I'm not scared,' she said, a tremor in her voice belying her words, 'but I am cold.'

'Then it's time we hit the hay.'

This was the part she had been dreading. Earlier, they had unrolled their sleeping-bags on the floor of the gloomy shed, disturbing spiders and birds which were roosting in the rafters. She would almost rather have slept in the open, beside the fire. But to do that would mean confessing to Robb that the woolshed scared her with its creaking walls and holes in the roof large enough to glimpse the stars.

Fully clothed, she crawled into the sleeping-bag, praying that no insect had made a home in the foot of it. Cocooned in the padded bag, she felt a little better and she watched Robb getting ready for bed. He really was a magnificent specimen of a man, all shoulders and massive thighs with no excess flesh anywhere. Raw-boned was a good description. A real mountain man.

Half asleep, she started when he leaned over her. 'I take my hat off to you,' he said softly, his expression hidden in the gloom. 'You must be sore all over after today's ride, but you haven't said a word of complaint.' Astonishingly, his head bent to hers and his lips brushed her cheek. 'Sleep tight.'

Before she could react he slid into his own sleeping-bag on the other side of the room and rolled, bag and all, on to his side, facing away from her.

She looked at his reassuring bulk and felt a frisson of excitement down her spine. His kiss had been brotherly and light, but it left a sensation along her cheek as if she had been branded.

She moved restively in the bag and suppressed a groan. He was right about her being sore. She felt as if she had been flogged, every muscle screaming for relief. But she was proud of not having complained, even if it was just pig-headedness to prove she could take anything Robb Wetherill dished out. He was proud of her! She absorbed the discovery with pleasure, tinged with wonder that his opinion already mattered so much.

Several times during the night her aching muscles woke her and she shifted, trying to find a comfortable position. The night was alive with strange creaks and rustling noises, and she heard the dingos howling nearby.

Each time she stirred, her glance went automatically to where Robb slept. Only the sight of his reassuring shape, outlined by moonlight, helped her to close her eyes again to try to rest.

When she next awoke, it was early morning and thin fingers of mist trailed across the sky below them. Below them, she realised with a start. They were as high as the clouds.

'Breakfast time, sleepyhead,' called Robb from outside the woolshed.

She almost cried out with pain as she struggled out of her sleeping-bag and her abused muscles came to protesting life. God! How was she to get on a horse again feeling like this?

'How are the muscles this morning?' Robb asked with maddening good cheer when she joined him for breakfast, moving carefully so that he wouldn't notice her discomfort.

'I'm, fine, thank you, just dandy,' she said through clenched teeth.

'Good. Then you're all set for the next leg.'

The next leg turned out to be even steeper and longer than the previous day's ride. Every time the horse's powerful muscles worked to pull them up the incline, she almost sobbed with pain.

She was on the point of begging Robb for a rest, her pride and her mission be damned, when he yelled excitedly back to her from further up the trail. 'Brumbies!'

Now what? Gemma strained forward and soon saw

what Robb was so excited about. Ahead of them was a mob of wild bush horses cornered in a gully.

Gemma had heard about the brumbies made famous in Banjo Paterson's poem, 'The Man From Snowy River', and she had expected to see skinny, starving creatures with poor coats and even poorer prospects.

She was astonished to find that the leader of the mob was a magnificent bay with shining black mane and wild eyes. It reared back as Robb rode towards it.

Gemma's heart was in her mouth as Robb approached the wild horse but at the last moment, he swerved aside, allowing the leader to take his harem thundering out of the gully to the beckoning valley and freedom.

So entranced was she with the spectacle that she failed to notice that she stood in the horses' path until Robb called out a desperate warning.

'Gemma, look out!'

In panic, she hauled her horse's head around and headed down the slope, realising as Kael gained speed that she had made the wrong move.

By then it was too late and all she could do was hang on for dear life as the horse plunged down the slippery slope, dodging fallen trees and hummocks of tussocky grass. Behind her, she heard the drumbeat of hooves, and dared not try to pull Kael up.

However her pursuer was not the wild stallion, but Robb riding like a madman until his horse was alongside hers on the difficult terrain.

Like something out of a wild west film, he leaned across at full gallop, and grabbed the reins, slowing the horse inexorably while he controlled his own horse with his knees.

Just as he brought Kael under control, and Gemma started to breathe again, an overhanging tree branch swept across her path, lifting her from the saddle. She hit the earth with a sickening, bone-jarring thud.

Winded, she lay on the ground as Robb wheeled both horses around and came back to her. Kael's sides sucked in and out with exertion and there was white foam on his flanks.

Robb slid off his horse beside her. 'Don't move, you could have broken something.'

Nevertheless, she struggled to sit up. 'I'm fine, really. Just winded.' She accepted the hand he offered and scrambled to her feet. 'Thanks for rescuing me. I've never seen such spectacular riding.'

'If you live in the mountains, it's all in a day's work,' he assured her gruffly.

'All the same, I'm grateful. I was terrified when I saw those brumbies thundering towards me.'

He frowned. 'Your mistake was in trying to outrun them. If you'd veered off into the trees, they would have gone safely past you.'

'Now he tells me,' she said wryly, grimacing as she put her weight on her bruised ankle.

'Are you sure you're all right?'

No, she wasn't sure. She was one throbbing mass of aches and pains from the hard riding, and now she had bruises to contend with as well. She would give anything for a long soak in a hot bath, followed by hours of luxuriating in bed. But admitting it would give him the excuse he needed not to take her to the High

Plains. She lifted her chin. 'I told you, I'm fine.'

He looked sceptical but nodded. 'If you say so.' To her joy, he added, 'There's a drover's hut over the rise. We'll camp there for lunch and give the horses a rest.'

Which meant they could walk the horses back up the treacherous slope. Gemma wasn't sure she could mount Kael again for a while. But walking was something she could manage, although every breath in and out felt as if someone was stroking a firebrand down her sides.

When the drover's hut came in sight, she almost wept with relief. It was little more than an ironbark shed with tumbledown roof, but it spelt blessed rest.

On the hut's sagging veranda, she dropped down thankfully, easing her bruised legs out in front of her. She felt as if the skin had been rubbed off the insides of her thighs. She looked up dully as Robb loomed above her. 'Up you get. I've done all the work until now. It's your turn.'

Tears stung her eyes but she averted her head so that he wouldn't see them. Of all the times to decide to be democratic about the chores!

Without a word, she accepted the billy-can he held out and trudged down the slope to a snow-fed stream he pointed out to her.

'I hate him, I hate him, I hate him,' she muttered over and over to herself as she dipped the container into the creek. Granted, she had insisted on searching for the lost plane. But surely Robb didn't have to make everything so hard for her? She wouldn't be surprised if he had deliberately herded the brumbies towards her to give her a scare.

Even as the thought arose, she dismissed it. The picture of Robb leaning over at full gallop to grasp the reins of her horse was indelibly imprinted on her mind. He would never endanger anyone deliberately. She was allowing pain and self-pity to get the better of her.

The thought cheered her as she returned to the hut where Robb was sprawled on the veranda, his long legs stretched out in front of him as if he hadn't a care in the world.

'What do you want for lunch?' she asked sullenly.

'You'll find sausages and damper in my saddlebag, and there's tea for the billy as well.'

'No champagne?' she asked sarcastically, forgetting that she wasn't supposed to be indulging in self-pity.

He seemed oblivious to her rebellious mood. 'No, sorry. But you'll find freshly brewed billy tea is as good as champagne after a hard ride like the one you had this morning.'

At least he wasn't trying to pretend it was an easy ride, she thought with some relief. She busied herself melting butter in the frying pan and frying the sausages to dark brown succulence. The delicious smell wafted over the valley and made her mouth water.

While the sausages were frying, she buttered wedges of damper, the tasty bushman's bread. Every movement challenged her sore muscles, but somehow she finished preparing the meal without giving herself away.

When they settled back with laden plates and mugs of steaming tea, Gemma was careful to choose a spot on the ground well padded with fallen leaves, to ease her protesting bones.

'How am I doing so far?' she asked after they had eaten in silence for a while.

'All right.'

Anger rose in her like a gathering storm. 'All right? After that demonstration this morning, when I could have been killed, the best you can say is all right?'

He tilted his hat off his forehead and regarded her with wry amusement. 'We're not given to lavish compliments in the mountains, Gemma Tate. All right is the equivalent of bloody marvellous up here.'

Wide-eyed, she stared at him as she absorbed the compliment. 'Well, if you meant bloody marvellous, why not say so?'

'As I said, we don't throw praise around lightly up here. For example, what you called spectacular riding just now was fairly ordinary by mountain standards.'

'You make your countrymen sound like supermen,' she grumbled.

'In a way, they have to be. Life up here is not so different from the way it was a hundred years ago. A man has to be able to take care of himself or he's dead.'

'The way I would have been if you hadn't caught my horse,' she acknowledged, chastened because she knew he was right.

'Maybe.'

She felt like throwing something at him. He had just saved her life with riding which was nothing short of heroic, despite his dismissal of it. And he had admitted that her own performance had impressed him.

Now she wanted to shake him out of his maddening, self-contained complacency which was so different from the showiness she was used to in the city.

'What do you say when you get really excited about something?' she asked, determined to provoke him.

He uncoiled his length from the veranda, dusting himself down, then approached her with slow, purposeful steps. Her heart began to pound uncomfortably. 'What are you doing?'

He towered over her. 'I don't say much when something excites me. What I do about it is another matter.'

To her astonishment, he leaned across her and cupped a hand under each arm, lifting her to her feet. She gasped as his hands connected with the bruises on her ribs, but he misread her reaction. 'I can see you feel the same way.'

'I don't ...' she began but was silenced when he captured her mouth in a sudden, totally possessive kiss.

His mouth was warm and firm. Close up, he smelled of an enticing mixture of woody after-shave lotion, eucalyptus oil from his passage through the bush and a variety of man and horse scents combined into one pleasurable mixture.

Her veins were already charged with adrenalin after the morning's excitement, so she had only a little way to go before her heart began to race and the blood rushed to her cheeks.

His body against hers felt rock-hard and she was startled by how quickly he reacted to her nearness. She turned him on, she realised with a shock, and the feeling was very, very mutual, she found out a few seconds later as her pulses speeded up and her temperature rose. A moment ago, she had been cool in the mountain breezes. Now she felt as if her blood were on fire.

When he released her and took a pace back, she stared at him in wonderment. 'Why did you do that?'

'You wanted to find out how I react when I get excited,' he said huskily. 'You excite me, Gemma Tate.'

'I ... I didn't mean to,' she said, at a loss for once.

'If you had, I wouldn't have responded,' he said. 'In my line of work, plenty of women give me the come-on. Some of them don't care if their husbands are near by. If you had been on the hunt, I'd have been much more wary. But you're not, are you? I caught you by surprise.'

'Yes, you did.'

'But you didn't mind?'

'I ... I'm not sure. It might make things difficult when we're together on the High Plains.'

He shook his head. 'We won't be, so it's all right.'

'What do you mean, we won't be together?'

'That's what I said. After two days of fairly easy riding, you're already a wreck. God knows what some really hard travelling would do to you.'

Her eyes blazed as she glared at him. Had all her heroic pretence been for nothing? She decided to call his bluff. 'I'm perfectly all right. I might have a few bruises from the fall, but otherwise I'm ... as fit as you are,' she ended triumphantly.

She should have known better than to challenge him, she realised wildly as he stepped closer. His arms enfolded her and she thought for a crazy moment that he was going to kiss her again.

But instead, he enveloped her in his embrace, splaying a hand across the small of her back and wrapping the other around her shoulders.

'What are you doing?' she demanded, distracted by the nearness of a mouth which made no attempt to contact her.

'I just felt a sudden urge to hold you, that's all.'

With a shock, she realised that he knew exactly what he was doing. As his embrace tightened, the pressure on her bruises increased. She gritted her treeth, unable to squirm free without hurting herself.

In spite of her resolve, tears welled up in her eyes. 'All right, you win. Let me go,' she capitulated.

At once he released her. To her horror, her knees buckled and she pitched forward. If he hadn't caught her, she would have fallen.

'My God, Gemma, why didn't you tell me?' he asked through jaws clenched tight with anger. Whether it was at her or himself, she didn't know. 'I wouldn't have touched you if I'd realised it was as bad as this.'

Dismissing her protests, he swept her up in muscled arms and carried her to the veranda where he set her down on a blanket, pulling a saddlebag behind her head for a pillow. When she tried to sit up, he pushed her back down. 'Rest for a minute while I take a look at you.'

Mortified, for he would now discover her secret, she lay back as he pushed her sweater and shirt up, revealing her bruised midriff. He swore softly.

When he reached for the zipper of her jeans she mewed a feeble protest, but he pushed aside her hands and rolled the jeans down past her knees.

She saw his eyes darken with concern as he saw the red-raw patches along her thighs. 'Is it as bad as it looks?' he asked.

She nodded. 'Worse, actually.'

'Why didn't you say something?'

She closed her eyes against the worry she saw reflected in his. 'I didn't want you to think I was too weak to go with you to the High Country.'

'You little fool,' he growled. 'This was a test, not a duel to the death.'

Over her protests, he fetched a tube of ointment from his saddlebag and applied it liberally to her injuries. She was torn between relief that the pain subsided immediately and a tingling sensation which was aroused by his touch.

As he massaged the cream into her skin, butterflies danced jigs in her stomach. She fixed her gaze on the veranda-post behind his shoulder to avoid meeting his eyes, lest he discover how his touch was affecting her. She told herself that he was no more than a doctor treating her injuries, but her body recognised the lie and defied her attempts to quiet it.

She was a quivering mass of nerves by the time he had finished and helped her to dress. Thankfully, she wrapped her hands around the mug of tea he offered her, so that he wouldn't see how badly they were trembling.

'I'm sorry if I hurt you,' he said. 'I only wanted to make you confess that you were unfit to go on any further.'

She accepted his apology with a gracious tilt of her head. 'You weren't to know.'

'But it was a fool way to find out. With your injuries, I might have hurt you badly with that bear-hug.'

He dropped down beside her and stared moodily out across the valley. 'Finding that plane wreck must be awfully important to you.' His dark-eyed gaze raked her intently. 'What I'd like to know is why.'

'It has the makings of a good story,' she said blithely.

He whirled on her, his expression thunderous. 'Don't give me that. Nobody puts themselves through an ordeal like this just for a story.'

Taking the mug from her hands, he set it aside, forcing her to face him. 'Now let's have the truth, starting with who you really are and what you're doing here.'

CHAPTER THREE

THERE was a long silence while his eyes bored into her like gimlets. There was nothing flattering in the appraisal. All traces of friendliness had vanished.

In its place was an atmosphere of such unrelenting coldness that she shivered. She had known he would find out the truth sometime but she had hoped it would be after he had come to know her. Then he might have given her the benefit of the doubt.

But she was not to have that chance. He shifted impatiently. 'Well?'

With little hope of convincing him, she tried again. 'I told you, I'm a journalist on a story.'

'A story my ... my aunt!' he exploded savagely, obviously tempted to use much stronger language. She flinched at the raw anger in his voice. 'Your legs tell the truth even if you don't. You didn't put yourself through two days of hell just for a story.'

'You're right,' she said, her tone defeated. He would settle for nothing less than the truth. 'I am covering the story for *Outback* magazine. But ...' she added quickly when he started to interrupt, 'I have my own reasons for wanting to find the wreck of the *Plains Drifter*. Jack Duncan was my father.'

In despair, she watched his expression change from curious to furiously angry, the gold-flecked eyes hardening. 'You bitch! You deliberately gave me a false name and duped me into coming here knowing I wouldn't have given you the time of day if I'd known you were Duncan's daughter.'

He spat the name out like an insult. 'I didn't lie to you about my name,' she defended herself. 'Tate is my mother's maiden name. The family adopted it after Dad disappeared, so that the media would leave us alone.'

'Which doesn't change the facts,' Robb ground out. 'Y~u must have thought this was a great joke, getting your own back on the family your father robbed.'

This was too much. She felt the colour rush to her cheeks as her own anger boiled over. 'I did no such thing. You're as bad as your father, Robb Wetherill. He believed what he wanted to believe and didn't let the truth stand in his way.'

Robb's lip curled into a sneer. 'You know what the truth is, I suppose?'

'I know my father wouldn't steal your people's money. He was making a good living as a-charter pilot. He had no need to steal.'

'Oh no? With the size of the sum involved, even a saint could be tempted.'

'I'm not saying Jack Duncan was a saint. But he wasn't a thief either.'

'How do you know what sort of man he was? Lots of people hide their true characters from their families.'

Her chin jutted out determinedly. 'I know my father was an honest man. And I mean to find the wreck so that the whole world knows it too.'

He shook his head. 'You don't stand a chance. Too many people have already tried and failed.'

'They didn't have my reasons.'

He studied her intently, some of the disgust giving way to grudging respect. 'True, they didn't. But why are you so determined to find the wreck now, after five years?'

'This is the first chance I've had. When my mother came back to Canberra, she was penniless. My uncle and aunt took the family in while Mum found a job. I had to support myself as soon as I qualified as a journalist, so we had no means of getting back here before this. But none of us ever stopped hoping there would be some news of Dad.'

'Don't you mean you kept hoping he would turn up with the loot?'

Ignoring the pain from her bruises, she scrambled to her feet and faced him defiantly, her feet wide apart and her hands clenched into fists at her sides. 'You're determined to believe the worst, aren't you? Well, you're wrong.'

Her anger was fuelled by the memory of her mother staring out of their front-room window, her shoulders slumped and her eyes fixed on some distant place in the Victorian Highlands. 'Last year, when Mum was told she had a fatal heart condition, she begged me to clear Dad's name if I could. To ease her mind I promised; now I'm keeping my promise.' There were other reasons why she was here, but she was too angry to tell him more than the bare facts.

'Very touching.'

She winced at the sneering quality in his voice. 'It's the truth, I swear.'

'I don't doubt it. I can imagine how everyone would react if your father really died in a plane crash on a herioc mission. It would show how you and your family were poor innocent victims of the cattlemen's malice.'

'I don't want to prove any such thing,' she said

wearily, some of the anger going out of her as she realised they were getting nowhere. 'I just want the world to know that Jack Duncan wasn't a thief.'

'What will you do then—sue us for victimising you and your family?'

She had never considered such a thing. 'Of course not. I don't want to gain anything from this except peace of mind.'

'Which would be best served by letting the whole thing lie,' he said harshly.

'Nevertheless, I intend to find out the truth if . . .'

'If it kills you,' he finished for her. 'Judging from the state you're in after only two days, it could well do just that.'

She turned away from him, her vision blurring. 'A lot you'd care.'

'As a matter of fact, I'd care very much.'

The softening of his voice should have alerted her but she was so astonished to encounter any compassion that her built-in alarms failed to sound. Her eyes widened. 'You mean you'd still help me?'

His hands dropped to her shoulders and the warmth of his touch reached her through her shirt. His eyes hypnotised her with their compelling intensity. Unwillingly, his gaze held her and she stared upwards, drowning in the warmth and blatant invitation she perceived there. 'Don't . . .' she said, not sure what she was asking him not to do.

'Don't what?' he asked, his voice husky. Before she could reply, he bent towards her and kissed her lightly, his lips grazing hers so that she wondered if he had kissed her at all.

'Don't do that,' she begged, still impaled by that

magnetic gaze. 'You don't mean it.'

'Oh, but I do,' he assured her and kissed her again for emphasis. This time there was no lightness about it. His mouth captured hers in a gesture of possession so undeniable it was like a brand.

His mouth covered hers, and instinctively she parted her lips in response. Warmth flowed between them like an electric current and she swayed against him. His hold tightened and he moved his body against hers so suggestively that she felt an answering stirring deep within her.

When he broke the contact and pulled away, keeping his hands on her shoulder, she looked at him with sensation-drugged eyes. 'Why, Robb?'

'Because I care about you. I want you to give up this insane idea and come back with me to Omeo. Nobody knows who you are. You'll be made welcome.'

His words washed over her like a flood of icy water. 'But Gemma Duncan wouldn't be welcome, would she?' she demanded, hating herself for her weakness of a moment before. It was all so clear now. He didn't really care for her. He was just using the attraction which existed between them to try to change her mind about looking for the plane.

'Now you're being paranoid.'

'Is it paranoid to want to clear your father's name?' she asked wildly. 'If it was your family, wouldn't you move heaven and earth to find out the truth?'

Her words had hit home. His mouth narrowed and the muscles worked at the edges of his jaw. But the shuttered look came down over his eyes and he turned away from her. 'You're a fool,' he said grimly.

'Then you won't help me?'

'What do you think?'

It was what she had expected but the words still struck her like a physical blow. It was too much. One moment he was kissing her as if she were the only woman in the world; the next he was rejecting her plea for help. Where had she experienced this before?

'I see,' she said dully.

Without turning around, he began to speak, surprising her. 'When Jack Duncan disappeared, there were two schools of thought in the highlands—that he had staged the whole thing to get away with the relief money; and that he really crashed in the widerness where the wreck might never be found.'

'Which do you belong to?' she asked, and found she was holding her breath as she waited for his answer.

'I'm neutral. I shouldn't be, considering that my father lost his cattle property because of what happened. After the bushfire, he had no more cash to start again and was forced to sell up. Now he lives in town, a bitter, lonely old man who vowed revenge on the Duncans for ruining him.'

'And now you intend to keep his vow,' she said, not phrasing it as a question because the answer was already painfully apparent.

'I don't believe in vengeance,' he said unexpectedly. But as her hopes flared, he added, 'But I can't betray him by helping you either.'

So that was the end of it. Dispiritedly, she gathered her things. The small sounds made him turn. 'What are you doing?'

'Packing to go back. Since you won't help me, there's no point in going on together. Your test is over. I failed.'

If she had expected him suddenly to relent and agree

to go on, she was in for a disappointment. Without a word, he went to the paddock where the horses were roaming and saddled them for the long trek back down the mountain.

Out of consideration for her injuries, he took the ride more slowly, seeking out the easiest passages, instead of the most difficult routes as he had done before, when he was testing her orienteering skills.

She knew she should be appreciative, but she could only feel despair that her hopes had been so cruelly dashed.

But what did she expect? Her mother had told her how the High Plainsmen had reacted when news of Jack Duncan's disappearance became known. Suddenly, the Duncan family were outcasts in a community where they had so recently been accepted. Their reaction was understandable. When money flooded in from all parts of the country to help the bushfire victims, he had been the logical person to fly the cash back to the High Plains. To people who had lost everything, Jack's disappearance was the final blow.

Ann Duncan stood the hostility as long as she could, hoping against hope that there would be news of her husband to silence the gossips. When no word came, she packed up and joined Gemma in Canberra.

Remembering how her mother's voice broke as she told Gemma about the accusations levelled against Jack Duncan, Gemma had resolved to try to clear his name some day.

She hadn't reckoned with an environment which was so hostile that she would be unable to explore it without expert help of the kind no local man would provide once it became known who she was. And she was sure Robb

Wetherill would waste no time spreading the news.

They camped overnight at the woolshed again, but this time it held no fears for Gemma. She was too anxious to be out of Robb's company. His cold silence and accusing glances were getting to her.

'Do you have to keep looking at me like that?' she snapped when she intercepted one such glance over a silent breakfast.

'Like what?'

'As if I'm some kind of insect that just crawled out from underneath a stone?'

'You're imagining things,' he said mildly.

'No, I'm not. Ever since you found out who I was, you've been treating me like a leper.'

'You didn't have to come back here,' he reminded her.

'Back to the scene of the crime, don't you mean?' she demanded, jumping to her feet. 'Well, I don't believe there was any crime, and I'm not afraid to face anyone.'

'Then why did your mother up and leave?'

She stared at him. 'She didn't leave because my father was guilty. She left because she couldn't take any more of the gossip and vile innuendoes.'

'That wasn't how it looked to my father and his friends.'

Suddenly, Gemma saw that he was right. By running away, Ann Duncan had only fuelled the belief that she and her husband were partners in crime. It would have been easy for them to imagine Ann and Jack meeting again at some agreed place to share the cattlemen's money.

'Do you think that's the reason she left?' she asked him defiantly.

His eyes clouded and his mouth softened so that she

imagined for a fleeting second that he felt some compassion for her, Then the softness was gone and the gold-flecked eyes were flint-steel again. 'No, I don't. But leaving didn't solve anything, did it?'

'Oh, for goodness' sake!'

She whirled around and hurried down the slope to the creek, needing to put some distance between herself and her tormentor. How could she ever have imagined that Robb Wetherill had a heart?

Reluctantly, she remembered the feel of his mouth against hers, and the tenderness of his touch as he massaged the healing cream into her legs. For a little while, she had believed she was attracted to him. It was just as well she found out in time what sort of man he was.

They reached Robb's house at lunchtime, but to Gemma's dismay there was no sign of her car. The mechanic had promised to return it to her as soon as it had been repaired. Evidently he had been unable to fix whatever was wrong with it yet.

A call to Omeo confirmed the bad news. 'I'm having some parts sent up but they won't arrive till tomorrow,' the mechanic told her. 'As soon as I get the parts, I'll put them in for you. Best I can do, I'm afraid.'

Miserably, she thanked him and hung up, dreading the thought of breaking the news to Robb that she would have to spend another night under his roof.

'I wouldn't impose on you if I had any other choice,' she told him stiffly.

'Too right you wouldn't,' he confirmed ungraciously. 'But since Doc Barnes won't be back with my jeep until Friday, neither of us has a choice. We're stuck with one another at least for tonight.'

'I could borrow one of your horses and ride to Omeo and spend the night there,' she volunteered.

He grunted non-committally. 'There's no need to be a martyr about it. I don't want you here and you don't want to be here, but we'll have to make the best of it.'

Was he suggesting a truce? 'I'm willing if you are,' she said, holding out her hand, a tense smile on her face.

He looked at the outstretched hand before ignoring it. 'I had something else in mind,' he growled. He picked up a bundle of fishing-rods which were stacked in a corner. 'I'll make myself scarce. That way, neither of us is inconvenienced. The house is yours.'

'When will you be back?'

'When I get back,' he said unhelpfully. 'Don't worry, you'll be safe here.'

Then he was gone, hefting a bag of gear on one shoulder and carrying the rods in his other hand like a rifle.

She watched him disappear down a slope, then sank on to a couch. So this was to be her punishment for deceiving him—a night in isolation in the middle of the bush. She didn't doubt that she was safe here, but the thought of being surrounded by nothing but forest for miles made her feel uneasy.

Why hadn't she told him the truth from the first? He would have refused to guide her into the mountains, but his refusal would have been tolerable when he was still a stranger. Now she had made the mistake of getting to know him on their two-day trek, and his rejection hurt so much more.

There must be other guides she could hire, she told herself without really believing it. What guide would agree to help her once he knew who she was?

Damn these mountain men! They were so narrow-minded and so sure they were right. Even the fact that Robb doubted Jack Duncan's guilt was not enough to make him want to help her find out one way or the other.

Robb saw his behaviour as just, she realised. His family had been devastated by one of the worst bushfires in living memory, then the loss of the cash meant to save them.

After Jack Duncan's disappearance, there had been a trickle of new donations, but nothing like the first amount. It was easy to see why the cattlemen were bitter and vengeful.

But what if it wasn't her father's fault? She knew that nothing less than the discovery of the wrecked plane would convince them he hadn't plotted his disappearance to get away with their cash.

Her head came up and a glint of determination lit her deep blue eyes. The thick lashes quivered over them and then widened to a forceful stare. If finding the plane was what it took to set things right, then find it she would, with or without Robb Wetherill's assistance.

'You're crazy, Gemma,' her brother told her when she telephoned him in Canberra that evening. 'You know it's a wild-goose chase.'

'I know,' she interrupted, 'I haven't a hope of finding anything after all this time, but I still have to try. I'm going to stay here until I find something, or until my money runs out.'

'What about your job?' Tony asked anxiously.

'My editor knows I'm here on a story, so he won't expect to hear from me for a few days. If it takes longer, I have some leave coming and I might be able to take it now.'

'You have it all worked out, don't you?' Tony said, his voice admiring. 'But don't take any stupid risks, will you? It's bad enough to think of one Duncan lost somewhere in those mountains, without you making it two.'

She shivered involuntarily. 'I don't plan on getting lost,' she assured him with more conviction than she felt. 'I've engaged a very good local guide who knows these mountains like the back of his hand.'

'I'm relieved to hear it. I hate to think of you wandering around there on your own. Anything could happen.'

'I told you, I'm in good hands,' she reiterated, excusing the lie which prevented Tony from worrying about her. 'Now tell me, how is your cadetship going?'

Her brother had decided to follow in her footsteps and had recently started a cadetship on a Canberra daily newspaper. At present, he was little more than a copy boy, but he hoped to become a political analyst one day.

They talked for a while about Tony's work and his studies in shorthand and typing, then he said, 'Kenneth was at the paper yesterday, asking where you were.'

So her editor hadn't yet told Kenneth where she was going. Still, she tensed. 'What did you tell him?'

'Just that you were away on a story,' Tony said and she breathed a sigh of relief. 'I didn't think you'd want him to know where you were.'

'No, I don't—and thanks.'

They said their goodbyes and hung up, but Gemma remained by the phone, her thoughts busy. Why was Kenneth asking where she was? After the way he had behaved recently, he knew she didn't want to see him again outside the office. He was one of the reasons she had been so determined to come here—one she hadn't wanted to share with Robb Wetherill.

Granted, she did want to clear her family's name. But there was a lot more to it. Kenneth was part of it.

She made herself some coffee, finding her way around Robb's kitchen by trial and error. As she sipped the steaming drink, she thought about Kenneth, the man she had believed herself in love with, before his true character revealed itself.

Kenneth Shelton was using environmental journalism as a springboard into politics. He intended to be the country's Prime Minister one day, he told her seriously. She believed him and encouraged his faith in himself. He was, after all, a dynamic and presentable man with a touch of John Kennedy in his appearance. There was every chance he would realise his ambition.

He had seen her as the ideal candidate for a political wife, she knew now. She was passably good looking with a suitable career of her own and no blemishes on her past to affect his chance of being elected to high office.

That was, until he found out about Jack Duncan. She had intended to tell him, but just never got around to it. It had seemed irrelevant to their blossoming romance.

She would never forget the day Kenneth stormed into her cubicle at *Outback* magazine. He was clutching a photocopy of an old newspaper story and he waved it in her face, his eyes blazing.

'What the hell do you think this is, Gemma *Duncan*?'

She was genuinely bewildered. 'What's the matter, Ken?'

He looked on the verge of an explosion. 'What's the matter? I'm dating a woman whose father was involved in one of the biggest scandals of recent times, and she asks me what's the matter?'

'Calm down, Ken,' she pleaded, stung by his tone. 'There was no scandal, as you call it, although the papers did make headlines out of it.'

'Next thing, you'll be denying that your father disappeared with thousands of dollars in donated money.'

'I'm not denying it,' she said with an impending sense of doom. 'I am denying that there was any scandal attached. My father's plane crashed in the mountains and was never recovered.'

Kenneth's face didn't lose its purple hue. 'That's not what the papers say. I only came across this story while I was researching something else. My God, Gemma, don't you see what a discovery like this could do to my political career if it came out after we . . . after . . .' He didn't even have the courage to say he had considered marriage to her.

'There's no need to worry,' she said in the same icy tone. 'Because it's over between us. If I'd known how you would take this, it would have been over long ago.'

By taking the initiative, she caught him by surprise, but he looked relieved nonetheless. 'I always thought Alan Tate was your father,' he grumbled.

'Uncle,' she corrected. 'But it hardly matters now, does it? Goodbye, Kenneth. Good luck with your career.'

He had stumbled out with almost indecent haste, leaving her to slump at her desk, more shaken than she had allowed him to see.

They had been going out for almost a year, finding more common interests every time they dated. They both loved politics and took pleasure in debating the affairs of the nation over coffee far into the night.

They had just progressed to a more intimate stage, when they could consider marriage. Even now, realising how shallow and selfish Kenneth's interest in her had been, Gemma still felt a sense of loss for the closeness they had shared.

How long was her past going to haunt her? She had asked herself time and time again. Kenneth's reaction was the latest in several such incidents which had marred the last few years and which she had never shared with anyone.

If Gemma's mother wondered why her daughter was so anxious to exchange her room in Uncle Alan's home for a bachelor apartment, she never voiced her concern. Maybe she sensed that there were problems between Gemma and her uncle. They started with his off-hand reference to 'bad blood' after she came home late from college on occasion. The comment stung but she dismissed it, aware that her mother needed her brother's support and unwilling to come between them.

There were other occasions when Alan referred to Gemma's father in some derogatory way. His 'what else can you expect?' when Tony got into some boyish strife needled Gemma as little else did.

Finally, she decided to move away without telling her mother the reason. She would go and take her bad blood with her, she decided, and had seen as little as possible of her uncle after that.

Her aunt and uncle were good to her mother, she knew, and she was grateful. But they seemed unable to accept the Duncan children as other than potential delinquents, no matter how hard they tired to please the Tates. Staying out too late, getting less-than-perfect results in their studies were all attributable to their genes.

Tony seemed not to mind Alan Tate's attitude. He was a more easy-going personality than Gemma to begin with, but she also suspected that he might believe Alan's theory himself. This worried her but she couldn't see what she could do to change matters, except by finally laying the mystery to rest.

So there were a lot more reasons for her presence here than she had shared with Robb Wetherill. She didn't want his scorn, or worse, his pity. She only wanted his help . . . needed it, she amended. And he had withdrawn it. So what was she to do now?

An alpine dingo howled in the forest outside and she shivered, getting up to switch on lights to shut out the gloom of evening.

There was no sign of Robb and she wondered if he would be coming back tonight at all. She didn't relish the idea of spending the night alone. Yet he apparently found the idea of her company so unwelcome that he was deliberately avoiding the house.

He didn't find it unwelcome last night, she thought unwillingly. When he kissed her, there was no contempt or derision in his manner. Instead, there was a reluctant fusing of their bodies, as if they could be physically attracted even while hating each other.

Was that possible? she asked herself. Could two people be as polar opposites as she and Robb, and still be attracted to each other? 'Opposites attract,' she told herself and gave her reflection in the night-dark window a startled glance. Was she attracted to Robb Wetherill in spite of everything?

Yes, she conceded reluctantly. He was the most

physically attractive man she had ever met, not chocolate-box perfect to look at but with a compelling virility that drew her like a magnet.

He was like one of the alpine dingos he had described to her—a combination of native mountain creature and domestic animal. She pictured him as a shaggy-coated dingo, poised on a cliff-top howling its message of defiance to the world.

Yes, Robb fitted that description. At the same time, she remembered something else he had told her about the native dogs. They mated for life. No casual affairs for them.

There was something else she should remember, she told herself, before she romanticised his attraction too much. He had also told her that a dingo kills for pleasure.

CHAPTER FOUR

NOISES in the kitchen allied to the tantalising aroma of freshly brewed coffee roused Gemma from a deep sleep. Her first waking thought was 'Robb's back', and she grimaced in annoyance at the feeling of pleasure the discovery brought.

Why should she care if he had finally deigned to return? There had been no sign of him all evening, although she stayed up till nearly midnight, listening to the soughing of the wind in the snowgums and the distant howls of the dingos. Finally, driven by tiredness, she had gone to bed.

That she had slept, soundly, surprised her. She had expected to lie awake waiting for Robb to return. But she had fallen asleep as soon as she closed her eyes, dreaming of wild rides through rugged ranges, and across alpine meadows carpeted with silver snow daisies.

She struggled upright, rubbing her eyes, then gasped with delight as she looked out of the window behind her bed. It was a breathtakingly clear autumn morning, the sky a brittle blue canopy over the green landscape. Outside her window, a flame robin chirruped out his territorial claim, and a family of ravens crooned to each other from the branches of an alpine ash,

The beauty and tranquillity softened her mood and her tone was gentle when she joined Robb in the kitchen. 'Good morning, isn't it a glorious day?'

His eyebrows lifted in surprise. 'I gather you slept well.'

The spell was broken. 'No thanks to you. I expected to toss and turn all night, wondering where you were.'

'I'm quite capable of taking care of myself in the mountains,' he said mildly. 'I spend plenty of nights out trout-fishing.'

She felt a flicker of regret that her pleasure on awakening had been spoiled by remembering their animosity, and some demon drove her to spoil his mood, too. 'Leaving your house-guest to her own devices,' she retorted. 'Some host you are.'

'I don't recall that was exactly our relationship,' he responded.

From the coldness in his voice, she had achieved her aim of annoying him, but she took no satisfaction from it. She was only sorry that they couldn't share the majesty of the mountains without personalities intruding. But he was the enemy. 'You made the rules,' she reminded him.

In hostile silence, he served her a breakfast of creamy porridge and freshly squeezed orange juice, but she only picked at the food, her appetite non-existent. 'You'll have to tell me how much I owe you for my keep,' she ventured dispiritedly.

He frowned crossly. 'I don't want your money.'

'But I insist on paying for my food and my room.'

He shrugged. 'Insist all you like, I still won't take your money.'

She dropped her spoon with a clatter. 'You are the most bull-headed man I have ever met, Robb Wetherill!'

'I can live with it.'

'Well, I can't. I believe in paying my way. It's how I was brought up.'

His eyes raked her, their expression disdainful. 'Then you must get it from your mother's side.'

This was too much. She jumped up and her chair crashed to the floor behind her. 'That's enough, Mister Wetherill. I've had all I can stand of your snide remarks about my father. He wasn't a thief and I intend to prove it, with or without you. There must be another guide who can take me to the High Plains.'

He ignored her outburst and went on calmly sugaring his coffee. 'No, there isn't,' he said with maddening dispassion.

'You mean you'll make sure there isn't,' she flung at him.

He eyed her contemptuously. 'I won't have to. I'm the only professional guide working around here this season. Most people prefer to work during the ski season when there's more money around. They head for the northern hemisphere during our summer.'

She was sure he was telling the truth. Miserably, she righted her chair and sat down again, cradling her chin in both hands. 'So that's that.'

'I'm afraid so.'

He sounded so apologetic that she studied him curiously. What a strange mixture he was. One minute he was scathing towards her because she was Jack Duncan's daughter; the next he sounded genuinely sorry that he couldn't help her to find another guide.

Any minute now he would apologise because his precious principles wouldn't let him take her himself. She wondered it if was worth trying another appeal to his good nature. Assuming he had one, of course, and she wasn't imagining these glimpses of sensitivity.

Before she could frame her appeal, however, the telephone shrilled, its mechanical voice sounding out of place in the mountain stillness.

She watched Robb as he answered it, noting how his body set changed from languid to alert as he took the message. 'I see. What time will it be ready? No, I'll pick it up myself. Thanks. See you.' He replaced the receiver and returned to the table. 'That was the mechanic in Omeo. He says your car will be ready by lunchtime.'

Although she should be pleased, she felt frustrated that her chance of persuading Robb to change his mind had slipped away. Soon she would have no excuse to linger in his home. 'Is the mechanic driving it up here?' she asked.

He shook his head. 'This isn't the big city. How would he get back to town?'

'I hadn't thought. Then what will he do?'

'I'll hitch a lift with my friend Nobby Davis, and drive it back for you,' he supplied.

'That's very kind of you,' she said stiffly. 'But why can't I just go with this Nobby Davis, pick up my car and get out of here?'

'Much as you'd like that, I need to go to town myself and bring back some fresh supplies. I have plenty of dried goods on hand but no eggs or bread. In case you hadn't noticed, you've made rather a dent in the groceries in the last couple of days.'

Guilt made the colour rise in her cheeks. 'I'm sorry, I didn't realise,' she aplogised again. Damn, this was getting to be a bad habit. 'But I did offer to pay,' she reminded him.

'You can't eat money for breakfast,' he said equably.

'But you're welcome to come to town with me, provided you don't mind driving me back here before you leave.'

Since it was her fault that he had to make the trip, she could hardly object, but she dismissed his suggestion with a shake of her head. An idea was starting to form in her mind and she needed some time to think about it. Maybe there was a way out of her dilemma after all.

'No thanks, I'd rather wait here. I . . . I'd like to wash my hair before I set off.'

His derisive look said 'typical female' but she let it pass. As long as he didn't suspect she was up to something, he would leave her alone and she could concentrate on what was fast becoming a plan.

Nobby Davis, it turned out, was a retired stockman who lived in a cottage a few miles up the road from Robb's house. In a battered Holden utility of uncertain vintage, he was making his weekly trip into Omeo for supplies.

When Robb answered his knock, Nobby didn't seem surprised to find Gemma in residence. He raised his battered felt hat courteously. 'Morning, missus.'

'Good morning, Mr Davis,' she said, guessing his identity. 'It's a lovely day.'

'It is that.' He turned to Robb. 'Anything I can get for you in Omeo, Robb?'

She turned away as Robb explained that he needed a lift to town. The bushman's acceptance of her presence made her wonder how many women Robb entertained in the isolation of his cottage. Somehow, the thought made her feel uncomfortable. Of course, he had a perfect right to entertain anyone he wanted. But the idea of him ministering to another woman the way he had tended to

Gemma's injuries brought an unexpected ache to her throat.

She started as Robb's brown hand came down on her shoulder. 'It's all set. Are you sure you'll be all right here until I get back this afternoon?'

She kept her elation out of her face. 'I was all right last night, and you weren't worried then,' she said tartly, anxious to make him believe her mood hadn't changed.

He grinned wryly, refusing to be provoked. 'I was never out of earshot of the house. If you had screamed, I would have come running.'

So he hadn't deserted her after all, but had only taken himself a short distance away, she thought in astonishment. Maybe he wasn't as indifferent to her as he pretended. 'Would you really have come running?' she asked softly, without turning around.

But the silence told her he had already left.

She forced herself to sit down and finish her coffee until she was certain that Robb wasn't going to return for any reason. While she waited, she went over the details of her plan.

A slow smile spread across her face. What would Robb do when he returned this afternoon and discovered that she was already on her way to the High Plains alone? He would have little choice but to follow her.

He could let her go, she considered. It was a risk, but one she must take. She would just have to make sure he followed her.

He was running short of fresh food, but had said he kept dried supplies for his expeditions in the house. First she had to locate them and pack enough food for at least her first few days of travel.

She was suddenly grateful that *Outback* magazine had

sent her on an Outward Bound survival course as one of her earliest assignments with them. She was going to need all she had learned about surviving in the bush until Robb caught up with her.

That she was being foolhardy she refused to consider. As a journalist, she was used to taking chances to obtain a story. This was no different.

An hour later, she had packed one of Robb's rucksacks with everything she thought she would need. Saddling Kael proved more difficult, but she remembered what Robb had shown her, and eventually had the frisky pinto ready and eager to be underway.

'Just one more detail to attend to,' she told the horse and returned to the house.

Working out what to say to Robb to make sure he followed her was more challenging. The note needed several drafts before she had one which satisfied her.

'Dear Robb,' she wrote, 'I hope you'll forgive me for taking matters into my own hands but I must know the truth about my father. I know it's risky and I don't expect you to understand but it's something I have to do. I am leaving a cheque for the supplies I have taken. I also took plenty of your special ointment as I think it will be a long ride. Thank you for everything, Gemma Duncan Tate.'

She placed the letter and cheque on his desk near his telephone answering machine. The bit about the ointment should remind him of what a novice she was in these mountains. Surely that would make him want to save her from her own folly?

Only when she came to mount Kael did doubts begin to assail her. What if Robb didn't follow her? She would be alone in one of the most inhospitable parts of Australia.

Luckily, her brief trip with Robb had given her an idea of which way to head, and she had borrowed a compass and maps from his desk. If she rode north-east she would be heading for the widerness region around Mount St Bernard where Jack Duncan's plane was most likely to have crashed.

Looking down, she was dismayed to find that Kael's hooves left no marks in the thick leaf mould which carpeted the forest. She would have to do better than that.

Leaning sideways out of her saddle, she began to break off switches of eucalyptus branch, leaving them dangling in a clear record of her passing. It was a trail a child could follow.

All the same, the hours passed with no sign of Robb catching up with her. As the sun dipped low behind a line of ghostly snow gums, their bark hanging in limp ribbons like Rapunzel's hair, she began to worry.

'Your boss won't let me spend the night out here alone, will he, boy?' she asked the horse, taking comfort from the sound of her own voice.

'Of course he won't,' she answered herself. 'He'll be furious at being tricked into following me, but he will come—won't he?' Her uncertain question hung in the air which she suddenly realised had grown thick with spiral threads of white mist.

Dismayed at the speed with which the mist was gathering around them, she was relieved to see the old woolshed looming up ahead. 'Thank goodness,' she said loudly, trying to dispel her growing sense of loneliness. 'We can camp here until the mist clears.'

It was too damp to build a campfire, so she unrolled her sleeping-bag and curled up on it, linking her arms around her bent knees in an unconsciously defensive pose. Loosed in the paddock beside the woolshed, Kael stayed as close to Gemma as possible, his head overhanging the split-rail fence.

Tony was right, she was crazy to come out here, she thought grimly. If the mist settled in all night, she was in for a very uncomfortable time.

Suddenly, a twig snapped somewhere in the white limbo beyond her campsite. She sat upright. 'Is someone there?'

The snapping sound was repeated, closer this time and she felt the hairs on the back of her neck rise. A tremor passed through her. 'I said, is anyone out there?'

Her voice sounded muted in the stillness. She waited tensely but there was no response. And try as she might to convince herself the twig had been disturbed by an animal, she had an eerie certainty that someone was out there. But who? Surely if it was Robb, he would identify himself. She tried again. 'Robb, is that you?'

The fear in her voice communicated itself to Kael who whinnied softly. She went to him and stroked his nose, grateful for the companionable feel of his coarse coat under her hand. Her eyes stayed fixed on the area beyong the clearing. 'It's all right, Kael, probably just some old possum heading home to his tree,' she said to the horse.

When minutes passed and no more sounds came, she began to relax, annoyed with herself for being so easily frightened. 'See, I told you it was a possum,' she said to Kael, recognising the comment as bravado.

This was silly. Who could possibly be wandering

around in a mist, miles from anywhere? 'No one,' she told herself firmly, and decided to prove it once and for all. If she gave in to her fears now, she was in for a long, sleepless night.

Suiting the thought to the deed, she fetched the billy-can from her rucksack and headed for the creek which she remembered beyond the rim of trees. The mist had lifted slightly so she knew she could find her way back to camp.

Nevertheless, she moved cautiously down the slope towards the murmuring stream, then returned just as carefully up the slope which was slippery with leaf mould.

As she reached the edge of the clearing, she froze, every nerve-ending quivering. There was someone in her camp. The unmistakable sounds of movement reached her ears. By straining, she discerned a very human shape bending over her things. 'Who's there?' she called loudly, sounding far more self-assured than she felt.

Instantly, the figure straightened and vanished into the mist. She waited a few minutes longer, her eyes and ears straining but heard nothing more.

Slowly, she advanced towards her camp. Had she imagined the figure? She must have done, or Kael would have made some sort of noise. She shook herself mentally, but couldn't quite accept that the intruder was entirely a figment of her imagination.

Then she saw them.

Leading to her sleeping-bag was a row of footprints, large and male, in the damp soil. Another shock followed the first. Her rucksack containing all her food and supplies was gone.

No longer frightened, she sank on to her sleeping-bag and rested her forehead on bent knees. Now she knew who her intruder was.

'You bastard, Robb Wetherill,' she called into the mist. 'If you think this will make me turn back, you're wrong. I'm going on, do you hear? I'm going on.'

Her voice died away, the echo muffled by the moist air, and she put her head down again. It was all very well to say she was going on, but how? With no food or equipment she wouldn't last another day in these mountains.

There was time enough to think about that in the morning, she decided, pushing the awful visions to the back of her mind. At least Robb hadn't been callous enough to take her sleeping-bag. She wouldn't freeze to death, and she still had the billy-can to fetch water. But water hardly filled her stomach, and she was ravenous by the time sleep overcame her. When she did begin to doze, she was repeatedly disturbed by bush noises which brought her to startled wakefulness after what seemed like mere minutes of sleep. It was the longest night she could remember.

Exhaustion must have taken its toll eventually, because the next thing she knew was the sun streaming into her eyes through a hole in the woolshed roof. She shaded her eyes with an upraised hand and squinted at her watch. It was after eight.

Her nostrils were assailed by the appetising smell of frying bacon and she smiled lazily. Robb must be cooking breakfast. God, she was hungry!

Then she sat bolt upright. Hunger must be making her imagine the smell, because Robb wasn't here and she had no food supplies left. He had stolen them all last night.

Her imagination must be vivid because the smell persisted and was accompanied by a sizzling sound. Someone *was* cooking breakfast.

She stumbled outside to find Robb crouched over a campfire, turning rashers of spitting bacon as if nothing was amiss. 'Good morning,' he said pleasantly, not looking up.

'Good morning?' she seethed. 'Just what do you think you're doing?'

'What does it look like?'

'You know what I mean. After leaving me to starve all night, now you turn up cooking breakfast as if nothing had happened.'

'Let's say I'm trying to make amends. Taking your supplies was a rotten thing to do and I apologise.'

The apology was so unexpected that she stopped in her tracks. 'Why did you do it?'

'I wanted to make you admit defeat. But instead of crying your eyes out, you rolled yourself up in your sleeping-bag as if you had every intention of continuing on in the morning.'

'Which I did,' she said evenly. 'So?'

'So I couldn't let you go on without supplies. Or alone for that matter. I decided if I couldn't beat you, I would have to join you.'

She could hardly believe it. Not only had she succeeded in getting him to follow her, she had persuaded him to help her in her quest. 'Then you'll help me look for the plane?' she said, her voice rising with excitement.

'I'll help you look, but I don't expect to find anything.

Too many other people have tried and failed.'

Dropping down beside him in the glow of the campfire, she smiled agreement. 'I know, but at least we can try.'

He registered her thoughtfully. 'You don't give in easily, do you?'

'No, I don't,' she agreed. 'I learned the hazards of running away when Mum left here to live in Canberra. If she had stayed here, things might have been different.' It had been Robb's idea, but the more she thought about it, the more she agreed with him. Running away had been the worst thing her mother could have done.

He accepted her reasoning. 'You're probably right. Still, stubbornness is no reason for getting yourself killed. You don't know what a risk you were taking, coming out here alone.'

'I wasn't really at risk,' she assured him. 'I did an Outward Bound course once, and I'm a keen bush-walker. And I had plenty of supplies.' She paused. 'At least, I did until they disappeared.'

He had the grace to look discomfited. 'I said I was sorry. If I hadn't been so furious when I got back and found you'd taken off, I wouldn't have done such a mean thing.'

She could imagine his anger when he discovered how she had tricked him. 'Then I apologise too,' she said at once. 'I couldn't think of anything else to do. When you announced you were going into town for supplies, I saw my one and only chance to set off in search of the plane.'

'You were very sure I would follow you. What if I hadn't?'

Now it was her turn to squirm uncomfortably. 'I

don't know. I hadn't thought that far ahead.' She smiled awkwardly. 'Don't ask me how, but I knew you would come.'

His brow creased in a frown of annoyance, but his eyes sparkled with amusement. 'Damn! I didn't know I was so predictable.'

Never that, she thought inwardly, but wisely kept silent. There was an unfathomable quality about Robb Wetherill, as if he had depths no one had ever plumbed. Outwardly, he was the macho outdoor type. Inside? She had a feeling there was a lot more to him there. Maybe losing his heritage and having to make his own way in life had something to do with it.

'Why so thoughtful?' he quizzed her when she stayed silent.

'I was just thinking . . . how lovely it is out here,' she dissembled. 'So peaceful and remote.'

'Yes, but deadly too. People have been killed here, after losing their way,' he warned her. 'I want you to promise me you won't go off on your own again.'

'I promise,' she agreed readily. Now that he was willing to lead her to Mount St Bernard, she had no wish to play the heroine. One night out here alone had convinced her of that. 'Did you get all your supplies in Omeo?'

He hesitated slightly. 'That wasn't really why I went.'

Her eyebrows lifted. 'It wasn't? Then why?'

'To see my father and talk to him about Jack Duncan's disappearance.'

She drew a ragged breath. 'He was the one who led the search for the plane, wasn't he?'

'Yes. I thought he might be able to give me some ideas on where to start looking.'

Her eyes widened. 'You intended to go on this trip all along, didn't you?'

Reluctantly, he nodded. 'Yes, but I didn't plan to take you with me. This country is too rugged for inexperienced people—bushwalking enthusiasts or not.'

'So you pinched my supplies to try and make me turn back. Of all the sneaky, rotten . . .'

He held up a hand, silencing her. 'I was trying to save you discomfort and possible disappointment.'

'You don't think the plane is out here, do you?'

'I didn't say that. The truth is, I don't know. My father was adamant that they'd conducted the most thorough search that was possible. He said I was crazy even to try again.'

'But you're going to. Why, Robb?'

He shrugged. 'Call it a hunch, whatever. It's just something I have to do.' He swept her with a searching gaze she found somehow disturbing. 'You realise you're in for a rough time, no matter what the outcome?'

'How do you mean?'

'If we don't find the plane, the suspicion remains that Jack Duncan made off with the Relief money.'

'And if we do?'

'There's going to be a body in that plane. Did you consider that?'

She had, more times than she cared to count. 'It's a chilling thought,' she admitted, 'but I think I'm ready. As much as one can be.'

He eyed her with satisfaction, as though she had just passed some sort of test. She basked in the warm glow of his approval. 'Good girl.'

They ate their breakfast in companionable silence, sharing the tranquillity of the bush at morning. Above them, glider-winged kestrels soared on currents of air, more graceful than any plane. Occasionally, a wallaby hopped away through the underbrush, and once Gemma glimpsed a porcupine, its tiny face peering out from under its coat of sharp quills. It surveyed them with startled button eyes then ambled away into the underbrush.

After breakfast they settled back on a carpet of leaves, to let their food settle and sip the last of their breakfast coffee.

'Would you really have pressed on without food or supplies?' Robb asked her curiously.

'Yes. Last night I was mad enough to try.'

He grinned. 'I can imagine. But why is this quest so all-important to you? I understand about wanting to clear your family name and so on, but surely that can't be so critical now you're settled in another city, with a good job. Your family background couldn't affect you any more, surely?'

'More than you can ever imagine,' she confessed. 'I didn't think it would matter and it didn't, at first. I was already living in Canberra with Mum's brother, Alan Tate, and his wife, while I finished my degree in communications. After Dad disappeared, Mum and my brother Tony came to live there too. That's when everything changed.'

'But you had property here. Your family didn't have to live with relatives if you didn't want to.'

'I'm afraid we did. Our land and house belonged to the air charter business Dad bought. It was mortgaged, and had to be sold after the crash because the insurance company wouldn't pay until the mystery surrounding Dad's disappearance was resolved.'

'So your father did have his share of money troubles,' Robb mused.

Her eyes flashed fire. 'It doesn't make him a thief!'

'Of course not, I'm sorry. I didn't realise how hard it was for all of you after ...'

'Yes,' she said shortly. 'It was even harder with people like my Uncle Alan making cracks about "bad blood" whenever Tony or I did anything untoward. Poor Tony, he was only sixteen at the time. At least I was old enough to move out and fend for myself.'

'Poor Gemma,' Robb said, sounding genuinely distressed for her. 'Was that why you wanted to try to settle the question once and for all?'

'There was more.' Taking a deep breath, she explained about her involvement with Kenneth Shelton. 'Everything was fine between us until he found out about my father. He wants to be a politician one day and he couldn't take the risk of having his wife embroiled in scandal.' Her voice grew bitter.

'I gather you care for this Kenneth quite a lot,' Robb speculated.

'We would have been married by now, if he hadn't found out about my father.'

'Which explains why you're breaking your neck to solve the mystery,' Robb said heavily. 'So that you can prove to him what a good little political helpmate you'll make.'

Why was he being so unpleasant all of a sudden? 'It isn't like that,' she assured him. 'I just want to get on with my life, knowing the past can't come back to haunt me at every turn.'

'I see.'

He didn't sound as if he saw at all. For some reason,

Robb sounded angry at what she had just revealed. What possible difference could it make to him? 'You're still going to help me in my search, aren't you?' she asked, wondering if his changed mood would alter things between them.

But it seemed not. He uncoiled from the ground and began packing things into their rucksacks. 'Yes, I'll help you look. I have some questions of my own about the disappearance of the *Plains Drifter*. So I can help you and your Kenneth Shelton at the same time.'

'He isn't my Kenneth Shelton,' she said irritably. Why did he persist in misunderstanding her?

'Whatever you say,' he said coolly, sounding unconvinced. 'We'd better get going. We have a lot of ground to cover yet.'

CHAPTER FIVE

KAEL'S hooves made clip-clopping sounds on the rounded river pebbles as Gemma led him to the water. The icy band of liquid was a vivid blue, reflected from the clearest of skies, and she sat back, absorbing the splendour of her surroundings, while Kael bent his head to drink.

A few yards away, Robb was also watering his horse but he did not look relaxed. There had been an air of tension about him ever since Gemma mentioned Kenneth Shelton. She was almost sorry she had brought it up. Robb seemed convinced that Kenneth was the reason she wanted to find the plane-wreck.

Nothing could be further from the truth. Kenneth might have meant something to her once. But she had no future with a man who wanted a perfect pedigree as a prerequisite of marriage. Charitably, she hoped that Kenneth would one day find a woman who could live up to his impossible standards, but she wasn't the one.

Lost in thought, she rode on after Robb, but suddenly realised he had come to a halt and was walking his big bay mare. 'Is your horse all right?' she asked concerned.

'He's fine, but we're just about at the end of our ride,' he explained. 'We'll have to leave the horses here and continue on foot.'

She looked around but could see no signs of human

habitation. 'Leave the horses where?'

'With a friend of mine, Joe McCabe.' Robb gestured towards a thick stand of alpine ash. 'He lives in a cabin among those trees.'

By straining her eyes she could just make out a small, gable-ended building made of vertical palings weathered to a silver green which blended with the trees. Only the iron roof and chimney stood out from the forest. 'I see a hut, but it must be lonely living out here,' she observed.

'Joe is rather a recluse,' Robb admitted. 'Eccentric, perhaps, but quite sane. He prefers the company of the birds and the animals to humans. There are quite a few men like him in these mountains.'

'How do they live?' she asked.

'They live off the land, fishing and hunting for their food. They might venture into town once a year for other supplies, or someone like me brings them a few things when we come this way.'

'I see.' She felt a growing curiosity about Robb's friend. 'What is Mr McCabe like?'

Robb laughed. 'You won't get far if you call him mister. He's Joe to one and all. As a matter of fact, you two should get on well, since you're both literary types. He fancies himself as a bush poet.'

Her interest aroused, Gemma followed Robb through the trees to a clearing which had Joe McCabe's hut at its centre. The bush poet came out to greet them and welcomed Gemma warmly. He was bearded and bent, dressed in an assortment of what looked like cast-off clothing, but he was neatly groomed and his smile was welcoming.

'How do you like the mountains, lass?' Joe asked her in his unusual gravel voice, leaving her in no doubt as to the warmth of her welcome.

'I love it,' she said sincerely. 'I've spent most of my life in the city and never suspected how splendid the remote parts of the country can be.'

Joe winked at Robb. 'You've picked the right sheila here, Robb, my lad. She'll make you a fine wife with an attitude like that.'

Gemma felt the colour creeping up her cheeks and looked at Robb in consternation. Since they were travelling alone together, Joe had drawn the conclusion that they were a couple. 'I'm afraid we're not . . .' she began.

'Not able to stay as long as we'd like,' Robb intervened, giving her a warning glance. 'We're headed for Mount St Bernard so we still have quite a way to travel.'

Subsiding into silence, Gemma glared at Robb. Why didn't he make their situation clear to his friend? Then she realised he was trying to avoid lengthy explanations of who she was and what she was doing here. Joe might not be so hospitable if he knew the truth about her. 'But you'll stick around for a billy of tea and some damper?' Joe asked.

They agreed and Robb loosed the horses into a paddock alongside Joe's cottage. The poet was happy to look after the horses, he said, and led the way inside his modest home.

'You must have been expecting us,' Gemma said when she saw the table already set for tea. A fresh loaf of damper was wrapped in a cloth, steam rising from it.

'You could say so,' Joe acknowledged. 'I didn't know who was coming, of course, but the birds and animals warned me that someone was on the way.'

How wonderful to be able to read the signs of the bush so accurately, Gemma marvelled. She soon relaxed in the company of the old bush poet, although she reacted uncomfortably whenever he paired her off with Robb, which was often.

'I'd like to hear some of your poems,' she said to distract him when he began to quiz Robb about their future plans.

Joe's eyes twinkled. 'Embarrassed about it, huh? I wouldn't be if I was you, love. I've seen more bush weddings and nippers born in these woods than you can count. With no doctor for miles, I've even brought a few youngsters into the world meself.'

Gemma blushed scarlet and looked away. Maddeningly, Robb seemed to find the situation amusing. He patted her hand indulgently. 'Don't worry, Gemma. We'll make sure there's a doctor on call for our brood, I promise.'

She gave him a withering look. 'When did you say we were leaving?' she asked, her voice warningly chilly.

He stretched reluctantly. 'I supposed we'd better be on our way. Thanks for the tea and damper, Joe.'

'My pleasure. I'll see you again on the way back then?'

'Sure thing. Come on, *darling*, let's get going.'

Robb offered her a hand but she ignored it, seething inside. When they were well out of earshot of the cabin, she turned on him. 'I suppose you thought it was funny, encouraging him like that? I can understand a poor old hermit mistaking us for a couple, but you didn't have to embroider it like that.'

Robb laughed. 'Poor old hermit, nothing! He was the one having the joke. He knew perfectly well that you dislike me. It was his idea of a lark to rub it in, and you fell for it.'

She stopped in her tracks. 'What makes you think I dislike you, Robb?'

'I suppose because you shrink away from the slightest contact with me. If it wasn't for wanting to prove something to your precious Kenneth, you wouldn't be here at all.'

'Stop calling him my precious anything! Kenneth was a mistake, an aberration. And I don't shrink away from you. I thought it was the other way around.'

There was a long-drawn silence, and finally Robb said slowly, 'I see. I suppose I've been giving you the impression I hold the past against you, just like Kenneth?'

'Well, don't you?'

He sighed heavily. 'I wish I knew. Part of me says if it wasn't for Jack Duncan, I'd be doing what I was born to do—running cattle on Wyuna, now. But another part ...'

'Go on,' she prompted.

'The other part just doesn't know.'

Disappointment flooded through her. She had been hoping he would admit to liking her for herself, even a little. But it seemed that her past was against her even here. Especially here, she amended inwardly. Robb, of all people, had the most reason to hold it against her.

How could she expect anything else from him?

At the same time, she did expect something more, she discovered. She wanted him to like and respect her, as she was starting to like and respect him. But what chance was there as long as the mystery still surrounded Jack Duncan's disappearance?

They walked along side by side in silence for a while, unconsciously adopting identical poses with fingers twined around the webbed straps of their rucksacks to keep the blood flowing into their hands. From previous experience, Gemma knew that if she swung her arms at her sides they would soon be swollen and uncomfortable.

Robb broke the silence first. 'Your father wasn't a cattleman. What made him come to the High Plains in the first place?'

The question was asked without malice, so she decided to accept it at face value. 'He was an engineer with a domestic airline in Canberra. He got his pilot's licence privately and was going to apply for a crew position, but before he could do that, he was made redundant at his job.'

Robb murmured in sympathy. 'It must be hard for a man of your father's age to start all over again.'

She nodded, remembering her father's tragic expression when he broke the news to the family. 'It wasn't his fault. The airline was trying to cut costs, and someone had to go. Luckily he had been with them for long enough to accrue a worthwhile sum in severance pay. Since he was too old to start again in another job, even supposing he could have found one, he decided to buy a business.'

'So he bought the old Sullivan charter business,' Robb finished for her. 'I remember when Sullivan announced he was retiring. With no airport in Omeo, we wondered how we would get on when we needed an air service.'

'The opportunity seemed like the answer to Dad's prayer,' she recalled. 'As well as the Cessna, there was the house and land with its own airstrip. Unfortunately, Dad had to borrow to complete the purchase, which is how it came to be mortgaged.'

'Didn't your family mind the upheaval, moving to another state?' Robb asked.

She shook her head. 'Mum could never refuse Dad anything. When she saw how much he wanted to buy the business, she agreed right away. Tony, my brother, was only sixteen at the time so he thought it was a great adventure.'

'And you?'

'I was doing a course in communications at college, so I couldn't leave. I moved in with my aunt and uncle in Canberra while the rest of the family came here.' Her voice became tinged with regret. 'I only saw the new place once, on holiday from college. The next time was when I came down here to help Mum after Dad disappeared.'

'Of course,' he agreed, his tone sympathetic. 'I only heard about it second-hand myself.'

Her eyebrows lifted. 'Where were you?'

'I was skiing competitively in Europe, as well as instructing, in Kitzbühl, Austria, when the bushfires hit the area. By the time the news reached me, it was all over. Then I heard that funds had been raised to help the cattlemen restock their properties so I thought everthing would be all right.'

'But it wasn't, was it?'

'Not for any of us.'

She fixed her gaze on the ground ahead, not wanting to look at him until the mist cleared from her eyes. It was true. Nothing had been right for them from the moment Jack Duncan was asked to fly the Relief Fund money from the various collection points back to the High Plains. The cash should have helped the farmers to get back on their feet and Jack should have been a hero.

Instead, his plane had disappeared without trace and an extensive air search had failed to find any sign of the plane. Everyone had drawn their own conclusions as to what became of the pilot and the cash.

She decided to change the subject before their memories overwhelmed them again. 'Is a ski-instructor's life as glamorous as it's said to be?' she asked with forced lightness.

His relief was ill disguised. 'Every bit,' he said cheerfully. 'A different girl every night of the week.'

How lucky for you,' she said sourly.

'Lucky for the girls, you mean,' he corrected her. 'There's a lot of competition on the ski-slopes to see who gets to date the instructors.'

'Easy come, easy go,' she quipped. 'No worries about getting caught permanently.'

'I'm not sure it's such a great advantage,' he said, his voice sobering unexpectedly. 'The ski bunnies only seem to want a good time.'

'But surely there are plenty of girls around who want

something more than a good time?' she asked.

'If they do, I haven't found one yet. Most of the girls I've met can't wait to get away to the big city and the bright lights.'

It was said as a generalisation but she couldn't help wondering if Robb was speaking from his own experience. Had he known a girl who preferred the city to life with him? Despite all that stood between them, she felt a pang of sympathy. They had both been unsuspecting losers in the game of love. It made her feel a curious kind of kinship with him.

The feeling persisted as they hiked deeper and deeper into the wilderness areas of the High Plains.

With Robb in the lead, sure-footed as a rock wallaby, they traversed wind-swept rock faces and mountain meadows of snow grass and tiny, perfectly formed wildflowers. Overhead, wedgetailed eagles soared and kestrels called, their cries lingering on the wind. At ground level, their passing disturbed wombats, kangaroos, spiny anteaters and a host of smaller alpine creatures.

At this altitude, the graceful snow gum which grew to fifty feet in height on the lower slopes was gnarled and stunted, reduced to bonsai-size on rock faces and in clefts. At every turn, stands of fire killed alpine ash stood as gaunt reminders of the bushfires which ravaged the area every few years.

'Have you ever been here during a bushfire?' she asked Robb.

'Once. After a very dry summer when the high temperatures last well into autumn. I was up here mustering cattle for one of our neighbours.'

'You were caught in the fire?' Her voice mirrored her horror as she had an unwelcome vision of him battling the flames.

He nodded. 'It was like a glimpse of hell. The whole world was burning around me.' He shuddered. 'I never want to go through its like again.'

'How did you escape?'

'I crouched in a waterhole, just a few inches of water but enough. Soaking a blanket to put over my head allowed the fire to pass over me.'

She could hardly imagine such a terrifying experience. 'It's a miracle you weren't killed.'

'Miracles are common enough in these parts,' he said tersely. 'We didn't lose the cattle that time. Somehow they managed to dash through the fire to safety.'

'You weren't so lucky the next time.'

'No. Wyuna lost most of its stock. They were yarded for transportation, and didn't have a chance to get away.'

So that was how his father had come to lose so much. 'Your house?' she asked softly.

'Totally destroyed. The only thing left standing was the dairy. The grass around it was eaten short by an old pet sheep we kept tethered there.' His mouth twisted into a grimace. 'You can't enjoy listening to this.'

Because her father had contributed to his people's suffering, she assumed. 'Should I feel guilty for bringing it up?' she demanded.

'Well, you must admit, it's an odd topic for conversation.'

'Maybe for you. For me, it's part of a family tragedy I lie awake at night wondering about. I feel the more I know about what happened here five years ago, the closer I come to understanding it.'

'You really believe your father died a hero, don't you?'

Her chin came up and her eyes shone defiantly. 'Yes, and not you nor all the cattle barons of the High Plains will make me believe differently.'

He regarded her with grudging admiration. 'I can't fault you for being loyal. But you're forgetting. I'm no cattle baron.'

Not any more. He didn't say it but his meaning was clear. 'It's useless,' she said regretfully. 'We'll never see eye to eye on this question.' Or on any other, she added to herself. He seemed determined to keep his distance from her by dredging up the past. It was hopeless.

She tried to tell herself it didn't matter; that he was only her guide, nothing more. Yet the feeling persisted that he could mean more to her if things were different. 'And pigs might fly,' she muttered to herself.

For the next couple of hours, she followed doggedly in Robb's wake, finding she had little enough breath for walking, far less for debating her father's character with him any more.

Gradually she became aware that the forest had grown darker and black spots were darting in and out of her field of vision. She blinked hard and shook her head but the spots persisted.

Ahead of her, Robb ploughed on, his strides long and sure, never once looking back to see if she needed help. It made her all the more determined to keep up with him.

A ringing sound in her ears blotted out the sound of

her footfalls on the leaf-mould underfoot. Her vision narrowed until she was walking in a tunnel of blackness, the metallic sound broken only by the harsh wheeze of her laboured breathing.

Something was terribly wrong. She stretched out a shaking hand but Robb seemed miles away. 'Robb, wait,' she called, hearing her voice sound ragged through the ringing noise in her ears.

Thank God, he looked back. Then he ran down the slope towards her. 'Gemma, why didn't you tell me?'

She tried to say she was fine, she just needed a few minutes' respite, but her breathing was too laboured to force the words out. She gulped the thin air and shook her head.

'It's the altitude. You've been pushing yourself too hard.' Robb forced her down on to a rock and pushed her head between her knees. 'Rest like that for a minute.'

Slowly, her breathing eased and the ringing in her ears subsided. Cautiously, she lifted her head. The spots had vanished. 'I'm all right,' she gasped.

He looked angry and anxious at the same time. 'You silly fool, you could have passed out. What are you trying to prove?'

'Sorry if I slowed you up,' she said angrily.

'There's nothing to apologise for. I'm used to hiking at high altitude. You aren't. It's nothing to be ashamed of. Here, these will help.'

He offered her some tablets and the water vessel. She drank from it eagerly. The liquid cooled her burning throat and the tablets slid down easily. After a time, her lungs stopped pumping like bellows and she began to feel normal again. She stood up on shaky legs. 'I'm fine now.'

'I can see that. Luckily for you, there's a survival hut over this ridge where we can camp for the night.'

'You don't have to stop on my account.'

He frowned in irritation. 'In case you hadn't noticed, it's getting late. I don't want to be caught out here.'

So he wasn't stopping for her sake, she told herself moodily. Then she chided herself. He was right. She didn't have to prove anything to Robb Wetherill. But she did have something to prove to herself.

The survival hut was a rudimentary structure of timber and corrugated iron, intended as a shelter for cross-country skiers and bushwalkers. Built at the turn of the century, it boasted lath plaster walls and a brick arch fireplace inside. The grating was black with many generations of campfires.

The furniture was rustic but comfortable—two chairs, a table and a timber-framed double bed. Only one bed, Gemma noticed, averting her eyes from it. There was a kerosene lamp for light, iron pots and pans for cooking, and a supply of snow-gum branches for firewood, stacked under the shelter of the iron-roofed veranda.

'All the comforts of home,' Robb commented as he shed his rucksack and stretched his cramped shoulder muscles.

Gemma followed suit, groaning as her shoulders protested at carrying the rucksack for so long. Hers wasn't nearly as heavy as Robb's but it was weighty enough to be noticeable after a while.

She watched as he made a fire in the grate, then put a

billy of water on top to boil for their tea. While he was
occupied, she went in search of a small creek she had
noticed behind the hut, and had a sketchy wash in the
icy water. She also lavished some of Robb's ointment
on her inner thighs. They were tender, but nowhere
near as sore as on the first few days out.

When she had finished, she turned back towards the
hut then changed her mind. Robb might appreciate a
few minutes to himself as well.

There was a hill beyond the creek, and she decided to
investigate it. Her tired muscles protested, but curiosity got the better of her. She wanted to see what lay
beyond this ridge.

The slope proved steeper than it looked and she had
trouble climbing the last few yards. By using small trees
as handholds, she was able to pull herself up to the top.

A cluster of moss-streaked boulders made a useful
perch from which to admire the view. She climbed
them carefully, keeping a look-out for the snakes which
slept in the clefts. From here, the valley lay at her feet,
green and lush, a garden of Eden where few people had
ever walked. Whatever her reasons for coming here,
she was glad to be among the few to witness this
splendid sight.

Suddenly, in the valley below the hut, a glint of
metal caught her eye. When she turned her head it
vanished. She moved her head a little. There it was
again.

At first she couldn't make anything out in the tangle
of underbush. But when she saw the metallic glint
again, she was certain she had found something.

Could it be the wreck of the *Plains Drifter*?

Barely heeding where she put her feet, she scrambled back down the slope and ran to the hut where a curl of smoke issued from the brick chimney.

'Robb, Robb, come quickly!'

The urgency in her voice brought him running from the hut. 'What's the matter?'

'I think I've found something. Come and look.'

Grabbing his hand, she urged him across the tiny creek and back up the rubble-strewn slope to the boulder where she had made her discovery.

When she joined her at the top there was no sign of the metallic glint but, by moving her head carefully from right to left, she caught the sun at just the right angle to pinpoint her find. 'There, do you see it?' she asked, her voice trembling with excitement as she guided Robb's gaze.

His reaction was more controlled. 'There's something there all right, but it could be anything. I wouldn't get your hopes up.'

But her hopes were already sky-high. 'Let's go and look now,' she urged.

He frowned. 'I'm not sure it's wise. It's late. Whatever it is could be much further away than it looks.'

'It could also be a plane that nobody wants to find,' she said tremulously.

His expression hardened. 'Very well. But I'll go alone.'

'Oh no, you won't. I'm coming with you.'

The determination in her voice convinced him she meant what she said. Without further argument, he led the way back to the hut and repacked his rucksack. 'We can leave the rest of the gear here and come back for the night.'

'After we look for the wreck,' she repeated.

'If it *is* the wreck.'

Robb was right. The place was further away than it appeared. It took them an hour of hard scrambling between the skeletons of trees burnt in bygone bushfires and through dense undergrowth before they reached the edge of the precipice where Gemma had seen the shine of metal.

'It must be down there,' she said, her breath tight in her throat. It was all very well to talk about finding the wreck of a plane. But the body of her father might be down there.

'I'll go down. You wait here,' Robb instructed.

This time, she didn't argue. All her eagerness to accompany him was gone. In its place was a cold feeling of dread at what they might find.

After what seemed an eternity, Robb's voice floated up to her from the gully below. 'It's all right, you can come down but watch your step.'

Gingerly she swung herself over the edge as Robb had done, using the tenacious cliff-growing plants for extra handholds.

She found Robb standing on a ledge below the cliff edge. He stood like an eagle about to soar from its eyrie on the swirling currents below, his legs wide apart and his hands braced on firm hips. At his feet was a snowdrift, perhaps twelve feet across.

'There's your metallic glint,' he said pointing to the blindingly white patch of snow.

'What?'

'There are pockets of snow like this all over these ridges. When the sun comes up, they start to melt and the water glistening on the rock faces is what you mistook for metal.'

Disappointment struck her like a blow. 'Melting snow, that's all it was?'

'I'm afraid so.'

All her hopes and fears dissolved into despairing tears which flowed as if they were never going to stop. She seldom cried about anything, but now she felt as if her heart was breaking. 'It isn't fair,' she gasped through clenched jaw muscles. 'It isn't fair.'

'I know, Gemma. You have every right to be disappointed and upset. It was an easy mistake to make.'

'You might at least try to sound sincere,' she ground out. 'Although this suits you much better, doesn't it? I'll bet you knew what it was all along.'

'Now you're the one being unfair,' he snapped back, his eyes bright with annoyance. 'From the hut, it looked metallic. It might have been a plane. I can't help it if it wasn't.'

'But you're glad it isn't,' she persisted, disappointment fuelling her anger. She knew she was hurting him but seemed unable to stop the cruel words pouring out of her mouth. 'If we do find the plane, all your theories about my father go up in smoke. So it's better for you and your self-righteous farmer friends if all we find is melted snow. Then you can say "I told you so".'

She leaned against the moss-covered rock face, cradling her face in one bent arm. The days of riding and hiking had taken their toll, draining her mental and physical resources. Now she had allowed her hopes to be raised only to have them cruelly dashed. It was more than she could bear.

Her whole body shook with reaction and she was astonished to feel strong arms go around her shoulders. Gently but firmly, Robb turned her to face him. 'I don't want to say "I told you so". Even if we don't find the plane, it doesn't mean anything. It just means our luck was out.'

'Then you think he might have been innocent?'

'I told you, I just don't know. Planes have been lost in these mountains for much longer than five years. The *Southern Cloud* went down in New South Wales and wasn't found for over fifty years. So anything's possible.'

He was just trying to comfort her, but she had a feeling he believed what he was saying. Just because the wreck wasn't located didn't mean her father had deliberately disappeared with the relief money. She managed a tentative smile at Robb. 'I'm sorry I was so mean to you just now. Thanks for trying to cheer me up.'

His hold on her tightened. 'I'm only saying what I believe. Why do you think I came with you?'

She had asked herself the same question often since they set off. On the surface he was the enemy. It was his father who had led the crusade against the Duncan family, resulting in their being forced to leave the area. Could Robb's views possibly be so different from his father's?

'Why did you agree to come?' she asked.

His eyes danced and his mouth shaped a teasing smile. 'A beautiful girl asks me why I want to be alone with her?'

'Be serious. I'm not beautiful. Why did you come?'

'Because I believe in justice. And because you *are* beautiful.'

His eyes captured hers in a gaze so compelling that she felt as if he was looking into her very soul. She shivered with the intensity of his inspection and his arms closed around her, drawing her hard against him.

'Robb?' she said uncertainly.

With one hand, he brushed the strands of hair back from her forehead. 'Sssh. I want to show you why I came.'

CHAPTER SIX

ROBB had kissed her before to try to change her mind about searching for her father's plane. This time, he had no such motive, so he could only be doing it because he wanted to.

It was a surprising thought, but even more startling was the sensation of his mouth against hers, warm and potent, coaxing a response from her before she knew how she wanted to respond.

In any event, her body made the decision for her, moulding itself to him with a fervour which caught them both by surprise. She was achingly conscious of every contour of his virile shape even through their protective clothing. The contact sent flames of desire racing along her veins. Though they were above the snowline, she felt feverishly hot. Yet his explorations were gentle enough not to provoke alarm. She felt only wonderment at being in his arms in such an unexpected setting.

When the kiss ended, his lips trailed away from her mouth reluctantly, as though an invisible bond linked them. He kept his face close to hers so she could feel the flurry of his breath on her cheek.

'This is becoming a habit,' she said huskily.

'Yes, it is.' He kept his gaze locked with hers. 'No matter how much I tell myself it's wrong, I keep wanting to kiss you again.'

Her mouth tightened into an angry line and she drew back. 'I suppose it's who I am that makes it wrong.'

He shook his leonine head emphatically. 'This has nothing to do with your family. I admit, it coloured my thinking when we first met. But the better I get to know you, the less it matters who you are.'

'Then what does matter?'

He gestured around them, at the soaring grandeur of the mountain ridges and dark, tree-cloaked valleys. 'All this. It's where I belong. There's no excitement for you here, no work for a journalist.'

'My work is important to me,' she conceded, 'but it isn't my whole life. And there are different interpretations of excitement.'

As she saw the shadow of concern darken his rugged features she knew she was right about some girl letting him down before. Why else would he be so wary of acknowledging the attraction they both felt? In time, she could convince him that she loved the mountains as much as he did. Yet she wasn't sure she wanted to, just yet. It was too early.

She forced a smile. 'You sound as if we have to make up our minds about each other right away. A kiss isn't a marriage proposal, you know.'

Instead of lightening, the shadows in his eyes deepened. 'No, it isn't.'

She had only meant they should take their time and get to know each other, before worrying about where it was leading, but he took her comment literally because he frowned and turned away.

He was once more the impersonal guide as he helped

her to scale the rock face, then led the way back towards the survival hut.

It was nearly sunset and the bush was bathed in an orange glow. The underbrush sprang to life with rustling noises as the nocturnal creatures emerged.

When she started at a sound, he touched her hand reassuringly. 'It's all right, we'll make it back to the hut before dark.'

It was the sort of reassurance he might offer to anyone. His words of comfort held none of the intimacy of his kiss. He almost seemed to regret making love to her on the cliff ledge. Was it really because he was afraid to risk another heartbreak, or did her father's disappearance still stand between them after all?

Robb had left a lamp burning to guide them back to the hut and they reached it just as darkness claimed the bush. It was peopled with strange shadows and eerie rustlings making Gemma thankful to go inside and shut out the night.

She couldn't shut out her own thought so easily, she found. Robb's kiss was still imprinted on her lips, and her sense of arousal persisted, so she was acutely conscious of being alone with him in the middle of the wilderness.

Unwillingly, she recalled every detail of his embrace, and she wrapped her arms around herself in foolish imitation of his touch. What was the matter with her? Anyone would think that she wanted Robb to make love to her, when it could only lead to misery.

She found herself wishing that things were different between them. If only there were no plane and no missing money, they would be free to enjoy each other's company. In a few moments on the cliff ledge she had glimpsed the heaven which could be hers in Robb's arms. Was that all she was ever to know?

Her eyes were drawn back to him. He sat pensively beside the fire and his shadow was elongated as if reaching out to her. Impulsively, she touched the tip of it with her foot. 'Do you think we'll ever find the plane?'

'Who knows? Just because we were disappointed today doesn't mean there's no hope.'

'Surely you weren't disappointed?' she said without thinking.

His eyes met hers in a searching gaze and the lines on either side of his nose deepened to chasms, giving him a satanic look. 'I know you don't believe it, but I *was* disappointed. Despite what you think, I do want to find the plane.'

'Why should you?' she asked in surprise.

'Let's just say I have my reasons.'

'Am I supposed to be satisfied with that?'

'As you like. I may be wrong in what I'm thinking. If I am, I'd rather say nothing than take the risk that more people could be hurt needlessly.'

Her anger flared. 'You're talking in riddles. We were the ones who got hurt. If you know something about the disappearance of my father's plane, the least you can do is share it with me.'

'I told you, not until I'm sure of my facts.'

Since he was obviously not going to tell her any more, she subsided into silence. Damn him! Who did he think he was anyway? She didn't need him to add yet another mystery to the many surrounding her father's disappearance. She began to regret responding so readily to him on the clifftop. He was still the enemy.

'Robb Wetherill, you are the most infuriating man I have ever met,' she directed at him in silent fury. At the same time, he was also the most attractive and formidable, she recognised. The memory of his embrace came rushing back and she felt her cheeks flush with colour. If only this expedition were over, she could leave here and not think about him ever again.

At the same time, this thought provoked a wave of acute and quite unexpected pain.

She started as he stood up and eased his woollen sweater over his head. 'What are you doing?'

'Getting ready for bed,' he said easily. Then he saw her heightened colouring and laughed. 'I see what you mean. Don't worry, I intend to unroll my sleeping-bag beside the fire. You can have the bed—all to yourself.'

She felt relieved and disapppointed all at once. Yet she hadn't really wanted him to suggest they share the bed, had she? She felt more alone than ever as she curled up in her sleeping-bag on top of the springy old bedstead.

It was more comfortable than the hard floor must have been for Robb, yet she was the one who lay awake long into the night, staring at the rough-hewn rafters and wondering at the havoc a kiss could work on one's senses.

How she longed for a leisurely soak in a hot bath, she thought as she washed herself in the creek next morning. The alpine air was too chilly for her to have a proper wash, so she contented herself with a sponge bath, wincing as the icy water connected with warm skin.

After her fitful sleep last night, her eyes felt puffy and gritty. They probably looked as bad as they felt. Robb hadn't commented when she got up this morning, but she saw him studying her speculatively.

'How long do you want to keep going?' he asked her as they ate their breakfast. She had volunteered to cook, producing scrambled eggs and toast over the rustic fire with creditable skill.

'Has my money run out already?'

'I didn't mean the money and you know it. I was thinking of your fitness to go on.'

So he had noticed her fatigue this morning. What would he say if she told him it wasn't due to the rigours of bushwalking at all, but to the confusion his kiss had created in her mind?

Although she had agonised over what his lovemaking might mean and how she felt in return, she hadn't reached any satisfactory conclusion. Frustration made her answer him more sharply than she intended. 'I'm perfectly fit, thank you. I can go on as long as you can.'

'You don't have to prove anything to me,' he reminded her yet again. 'Why don't you go back and wait for me at Joe's place? I can continue the search alone.'

She looked at him in surprise. 'You would do that for me?'

'For myself as well. Now I've started this thing, I want to see it through.'

'Do you always finish what you start?' she asked, thinking of last night's kiss. If it was the start of something for them, where would it end?

'I try to,' he asserted. 'Will you agree to turn back?'

'No,' she said emphatically. 'I also like to finish what I start.'

There, he could take that any way he liked! He gave her a look of reluctant admiration. 'In that case, why are we wasting time?'

There was work to be done before they could leave, however. The cooking pots had to be scoured clean in the river, the hut swept, then the pile of firewood replenished. This involved walking the hills around the hut, collecting dead tree branches and stacking them with the rest under the veranda roof.

When they had gathered all the loose branches they could, Robb set out timber tramlines to the nearest dead tree. In the hut was a sharp bow saw, which he used to cut all the dead branches within reach, then Gemma bowled them along the tramlines back to the hut.

'This must be what life was like for the pioneers,' Gemma gasped when they finally took a coffee-break. They relaxed side by side on the timbered veranda floor, surveying their handiwork with satisfaction.

'I think they had it a little rougher,' Robb observed. 'Snowed in for weeks on end. Battling bushfires in the summer. Eking out a living in between.'

She gave him a curious glance. 'You sound as if you know something about it.'

'My grandparents built a place like this at the turn of the century.' He gestured over his shoulder to the hut. 'As a child, I visited them once or twice and I can still remember the night their kitchen caught fire. We thought the whole house would go up. Everybody grabbed buckets and filled them from the bathtub, then emptied them on the fire. It was early spring and the water froze as it splashed out of the buckets. But they saved the house.'

She was beginning to understand Robb's attachment to the High Plains. 'Were your grandparents the founders of Wyuna?' she asked.

'Yes. They drove their first herd of Herefords up from New South Wales to start the place off. They lived all their lives in some part of the Snowy River Valley.'

She felt a pang as she realised how deep his roots went in this place. It was very different from her own family's varied history, starting with a generation of shopkeepers in colonial Sydney, to public servants in Canberra, before her father's ill-fated attempt to run the air-charter service in the High Plains.

How would it feel to have a century of history in one place behind you? For a moment, she envied Robb until she remembered what had happened. 'Now I understand why you resent me as much as you do,' she admitted, hardly aware of having spoken aloud.

He linked his fingers and cupped his hands behind his head, staring out across the valley. 'I don't resent you,' he denied. 'I resent losing something I valued very much. I took it for granted that I would inherit Wyuna and I dreamed of making it the finest cattle property in the High Plains. But I don't blame you because it's gone. Any more than I can blame the bushfires which were the beginning of the end.'

He was being scrupulously fair, more than she had been to him at times, and she felt a pang of conscience. 'All the same, if the relief money had reached your father, you would still own Wyuna, wouldn't you?'

His eyes blazed with a sudden fierce expression. 'We don't know that.'

Before she could ask him to elaborate, he jumped up and began to gather their things together, ready to move on. But his last comment lingered in her mind, troubling her. Ever since her father's disappearance, she had taken it for granted that the relief money would have saved Mr Wetherill having to sell Wyuna. Was there more to the story than she had been told?

But Robb was in no mood to answer the questions buzzing in her tired brain. He strode ahead down the bush track, shouldering his rucksack as if it weighed next to nothing, leaving her to struggle in his wake.

She had asked for this, she reminded herself when it became an effort to put one foot in front of the other. Robb had given her the chance to go back and wait for him at Joe McCabe's hut. Maybe she should have gone. She was only going to slow Robb down if she couldn't do better than this.

At more than six thousand feet above sea level, they were already higher than the ski resorts of Falls Creek and Mount Hotham. They had left most of the landmarks behind. Ahead lay virgin bush, little known and seldom visited except by the cattle which roamed the High Country in spring and summer. Here, a plane could lie undiscovered for years.

They stopped for a sandwich lunch beside a picture-book river where deep pools alternated with shallow stretches where small trout jumped almost at their feet.

Robb unpacked his fishing-gear.

'Do you think you'll catch something?' she asked.

'If I don't, we won't be eating tonight,' he assured her curtly.

She decided to leave him to his fishing, hoping it would improve his mood. Since they were likely to be here for some time, she decided to explore.

It was heaven to walk around without the heavy pack on her back, replaced by a jacket tied casually around her shoulders in case of a sudden chill.

Mindful of how easy it would be to get lost, Gemma took careful note of her path away from the creek, using the plop and whirr of Robb's fishing lure, as he cast and recast it into the pools, to give her a sense of direction.

The mountains were so different from the flat, dry plains surrounding her home city of Canberra. Here, there was snow for six months of the year. Many of the wildflowers and grasses were found nowhere else in Australia.

She could see why Robb loved this land. It was stark and forbidding but still strikingly beautiful. The trees were mainly eucalypts—ash, silvertop and snow gum, bent and twisted into fantastic shapes by the alpine winds. Their smooth bark was a painter's palette of green, orange, red and purple which would become even more pronounced with the approach of winter.

Sitting with her back braced against a snow gum, she wondered about Robb's cryptic remark that he wasn't sure the loss of the relief money was the reason his father had lost Wyuna. If there was another reason, it meant his father had persecuted an innocent family. Was that the reason for Robb's ambivalent attitude?

Wandering further, she came to a bluff which overlooked a valley of such natural beauty that she stood, spellbound. The twisted trees clung to the earth by tenacious roots and grew right to the edge of the jagged moss-covered rocks.

The rocks were a fantastic jumble of grey-green, some squared off like man-made columns, others piled on top of each other as if some natural upheaval had thrown them around like toys.

Below her stretched a shelf of rock where trees grew at right-angles to the valley floor, shrouded in greenery far below.

As she drank in the beauty of the lonely gorge, a flash suddenly caught her eye and she almost laughed aloud. She wasn't going to be taken in by another patch of melting snow.

All the same, she strained forward as the sun glinted off the patch again. It looked like metal. But it must be snow, she told herself, turning away.

As she spun around, her foot caught in a tangled tree root and she sprawled headlong, grabbing for a handhold to save herself. She missed and felt herself slipping on the mossy surface, over the edge. 'Robb! He-e-elp!' she screamed, hearing the sound echo down the valley.

She was conscious of trees and rocks tearing at her clothes as she slid helplessly downwards. Shale bounced all around her, dislodged by her passage.

Then her fall was arrested with sickening suddenness, when her clothes caught on one of the trees growing out across the valley. There was an ominous creaking sound but the tree held. She was a couple of feet above the ledge she had glimpsed from the top.

'Gemma, for God's sake don't move.'

She looked up to see Robb leaning over the edge, his face set in horrified lines.

'I wasn't planning to,' she said shakily. 'But this tree won't hold me for long.' As if to prove her point, it creaked again and she slipped a little further.

'Can you reach the ledge with your foot?' he asked.

Gingerly, she reached with her right leg, feeling the reassuring hardness of rock under her toe. 'Just,' she confirmed.

'Very slowly, see if you can inch your way on to the ledge. You'll be safe there and I can come down on a rope to get you.'

Manoeuvring herself from the tree to the ledge was harder than she expected but she managed it by the simple expedient of closing her eyes and throwing herself backwards, knowing as she connected with the cliff face that she was safe, at least for the moment.

'Good girl,' Robb called approvingly from above.

He disappeared for a few minutes but reappeared just as she began to get anxious. 'I've tied a rope around the trees further back,' he explained, and dropped one end down to her. It dangled a foot above her head.

Then Robb snaked down the rope and dropped the last few feet to the ledge beside her. 'Are you all right?' She nodded. 'Winded and shaken, but otherwise fine.'

He looked relieved. 'When I heard you scream, I thought you'd fallen to your death.'

'So did I,' she said. 'If it hadn't been for the trees growing out of this ledge . . .' she shuddered, picturing the outcome.

He took her in his arms and stroked the hair away from her eyes. 'Don't think about it. You're safe now. As soon as you get your breath back, we'll climb up the rope.'

She looked at the slender lifeline uncertainly. 'I've never done anything like that.'

'Piece of cake. I'll guide you every step of the way. But not yet. First get your strength back, then we'll try it.'

He dropped to the ledge and wrapped his arms around his bent knees. 'I've never explored this valley before. It's quite spectacular.'

'It looked better from the top,' she joked, dropping down beside him. 'But you're right, it is lovely, like a garden of Eden when the world was new.'

'I can see why you were so mesmerised you lost your footing,' he observed.

She spoke without thinking. 'It wasn't the scenery which distracted me. I thought I saw something down there, but it was probably another patch of snow.'

'Where?' He followed her pointing finger to a section of the valley floor which was much closer now. 'There is something shining down there.'

She suppressed the hope which rose within her, not wanting to risk a second disappointment. 'Do you think it's anything important?'

He seemed lost in thought. 'Maybe. I'm going down to take a look.' He stood up, brushing the dust off his moleskin trousers.

'Then I'm coming with you.'

His look said he would prefer to argue, but she faced him determinedly, legs apart and hands braced on hips, daring him to refuse her. 'All right,' he said at last, 'but you must promise to do exactly what I tell you.'

'You're the expert,' she agreed readily. She didn't

want to risk a repeat of her fall. Maybe next time she wouldn't be so lucky.

Choosing his hand and footholds with great care, and testing each one before he moved to the next, Robb made his way down the rock face like a crab, moving sideways then down. Gemma followed him, putting her feet and hands where he did, until they were both within jumping distance of the valley floor.

It was much cooler down here, and quiet, with no birdcalls to disturb the primeval silence. Automatically she dropped her voice to a whisper. 'I think I saw something metallic over that way.'

He nodded, sharing her reverence for the place. 'Let's go. Unless you'd rather wait here.'

She gave him a withering look and he shrugged, then led the way down the valley. Their footfalls were muffled by a thick carpet of leaf-mould.

Gemma's heartbeat sounded loud in her ears as she followed him. She told herself it was the altitude making her breathing so difficult, but she knew it was much more. This time, she had a feeling they were going to find something. Could it be the wreck of her father's plane? Her father's grave, she reminded herself, shivering.

At first it was hard to make out anything in the gloom. If they hadn't been looking for a wreck, they would never have found it, so well was the plane concealed in its hillside grave where the alpine sun never shone.

Digging into the metre-thick leaf-mould, ash, charcoal and earth which covered the object, they came to a network of rusted metal interlaced with thin sapling poles. The metal was twisted like an old windmill rig.

For a moment, she wondered if they had found an abandoned mine-shaft.

But after patiently sifting through the debris, Robb uncovered a petrol-tank cap, a stamped engine-part and a piece of metal with a serial number on it. He placed the relics on a moss-covered rock, not looking at Gemma.

'Is it the *Plains Drifter*?' Gemma asked, her voice tight with strain.

'Look.' He pointed to a blackened strip of metal on which was written the plane's name in cracked and faded lettering. 'There's no doubt about it.'

By unspoken agreement, they stood alongside the name for a few minutes in silent homage to her pilot. Gemma felt tears prick her eyes and she thought about the gallant man who had died in this wreckage.

Hearing her choked sob, Robb gave her a questioning glance. 'Do you want to stop?'

'No,' she breathed. 'We came to find out the truth.'

'Very well. But I want you out of the way in case this thing caves in. Go and sit over there until I call you.'

She knew he was fearful that she would stumble across her father's body, and wanted her out of sight when he found it, but she felt no inclination to argue this time. She didn't know how she would react to such a find.

Watching Robb was almost as agonising, as he uncovered the wreck with painstaking care. She wanted to scream at him to hurry up, but recognised that his care was necessary. The wreck had lain untouched for five years. It was so brittle that any sudden moves might destroy the very evidence they were seeking.

After what seemed an eternity, Robb had pulled away most of the debris covering the cockpit of the crashed

Cessna 310. Gemma saw him pause, then continued stripping the undergrowth from the plane's fuselage. It was in two pieces, the centre gaping and torn. He disappeared into the hole.

When he emerged, he was covered in moss and leaf mould. And his expression was grim.

'What did you find?' Gemma asked, fearing the worst.

'Nothing.'

She stared at him in disbelief. 'Nothing?'

'No body, no money. Nothing. Except this.' He held up an old, weather-stained leather briefcase. 'The money must have been in here.'

She crammed her hands against her mouth to stop herself from screaming. Above all else, this was the discovery she had feared the most. 'There's no sign of Dad?'

Robb shook his head, his eyes dark.

'Maybe he was injured in the crash. Maybe he crawled away from here and died somewhere nearby. Maybe he . . .'

Robb shook her so hard her teeth rattled and she fought for control. 'Stop it!' he ordered. 'There's no maybe about it. There's only one explanation for what happened here.'

She stared at him, her sobs drying in the face of his remorseless logic.

'Your father crashed the plane all right, whether by accident or on purpose we'll never know. But he didn't crawl away from here. There are no bloodstains anywhere in the cockpit, which is intact. He walked away. With the money.'

'Oh, God!'

Her sobs became tears of such anguish that she couldn't contain them any longer. Her father was all the things they said he was—a fraud and a thief. He had collected a fortune in cash meant for the stricken cattlemen of the High Plains, and had disappeared with it.

'I'm sorry it turned out like this,' Robb said when her sobs at last began to subside.

She looked up at him through misty eyes. 'You're sorry? I thought you'd be glad, Robb Wetherill. You were right after all.'

'Do you think the discovery gives my any pleasure?'

'How should I know what to think? A few minutes ago, I believed that my father was a good man who was only trying to help and died in the attempt. Now, it looks as though you were right. He stole the money and disappeared, leaving everyone to think he died in a plane crash. It seems so—so ...'

'Callous? Unfeeling?'

'Yes, if you insist. How could he do this to us?'

What she really meant was how could her father do such a thing to his daughter. In the midst of her despair, she recognised that some of her tears were for herself, deserted by a father who was so different from the man she thought she knew. Maybe her Uncle Alan was right after all. She and Tony did have bad blood. She felt tainted by their discovery.

She flinched when Robb rested his hands on her shoulders. 'It isn't the end of the world, you know.'

'Isn't it? How would you feel, finding out that your father was a thief? Worse, that the people he robbed were victims of a disaster and he was their last hope?'

His expression hardened. 'I'd feel the way you do. Betrayed, disillusioned. Hurt. I'd want to tear somebody apart with my bare hands.'

It was exactly how she felt. How could he know so precisely? She turned aside. 'Let's get out of here.'

'I want to go over the wreck first and make sure I haven't missed anything important. You don't have to watch if you'd rather not.'

She wished he wouldn't be so gentle with her. His anger had been easier to bear because it made more sense. 'What do you expect to find?' she asked dully.

'Some clue as to what happened here.' He indicated an area of metal shredded outwards around one of the engines. 'It looks as if some kind of explosion brought the plane down.'

'An accident?' she asked.

'Most likely. Turbulent weather developed around here after the *Plains Drifter* set off from Bairnsdale. My guess is, the plane was struck by lightning which caused the explosion.'

It was all so neat and dispassionate it was hard to remember they were talking about a crash which involved her father. 'How could he have walked away?'

'That's the part I don't understand. The cockpit survived intact, so it must have shielded him from the worst of the impact, but it's a long walk out of here through rugged country with few provisions, unless he had some on board.'

'You mean unless he planned something like this?' she said, her voice trembling with emotion.

'Will you stop casting me as the villain?' Robb said

irritably. 'I didn't imply any such thing. Lots of planes carry emergency provisions.'

'I'm sorry,' she whispered. The strain was beginning to tell and she felt the colour drain from her face. She swayed and would have fallen if Robb hadn't caught her.

He eased her on to a rock. 'Take it easy. This must be quite a shock to you.'

Her vision blurred. 'I could have handled almost anything but ... this.' She stared at Robb, her pupils large and black.

'Do you realise, this means he's alive somewhere ... out there?'

'I know.'

She tugged at his arm. 'I have to find him. Whatever he's done, he's still my father.'

Robb regarded her sadly. 'This is rough on you, isn't it? One minute, you think he's dead, the next you discover he's alive. But you shouldn't count on finding him.'

'Why not?'

His breath escaped in a long hissing sigh. 'He's been missing for too long. He might not want to be found.'

CHAPTER SEVEN

He doesn't want to be found. He doesn't want to be found.
The phrase haunted Gemma throughout the tortuous
climb back up the cliff face.

Could it be true? Had her father deliberately staged
his disappearance without a thought for the effect it
would have on his family or on the farmers who were
depending on him?

It seemed to be the only explanation possible. She felt
as if she was living in a nightmare as she ploughed
through the bush after Robb. Even the saplings
whipping into her face failed to distract her from her
tormented thoughts. Her father was everything they
said he was—a thief and a con-man. He wasn't dead but
allowed them to believe that he was so that he could
escape and live of his ill-gotten gains.

Where? How? The questions nagged at her. Although
she told herself that she didn't care, her heart recognised
the lie for what it was. No matter what he had done, he
was still her father. Somehow, she had to find him.

'Are you sure you're all right?'

She hadn't realised she'd fallen so far behind until
Robb paused and looked anxiously back at her.

She quickened her pace. 'I'm still a bit shaken after
that fall, but I'll be all right. Have we much further to
go?'

'Not much. Didn't you notice how far you'd walked
when you set off?'

She pushed the hair out of her eyes. 'Apparently not. It certainly didn't seem this far when I came the other way.'

'Would you like me to carry you?'

'No, I can walk, thanks,' she said a little too quickly. The memory of his kiss was too fresh in her mind for her to want to trust herself in his arms. All the same, as her aching limbs became steadily more sluggish, she was tempted to accept his offer. In her present state of mind, she longed to be held close to him and shielded from her troubled thoughts by his reassuring presence.

He accepted her refusal with a curt nod, but as she began to falter, he took her arm and supported her. Even this slight contact was enough to send waves of sensation surging along her arm and down her body. Feeling the effect of a mere touch, she was glad she hadn't let him carry her. They were on opposite sides, she reminded herself. Now that her father's guilt was in no doubt, she would be mad to let Robb get any closer to her. It would make the inevitable parting so much harder when it came.

Just when Gemma had decided she couldn't walk another step, they emerged into the clearing beside the creek where Robb had set up their camp. This time there was no question of sharing the chores. She was incapable of doing more than collapsing on to the grass, her back against a tree. As Robb moved around the camp, she stirred ineffectually but he gestured for her to remain where she was. 'I'll take care of things. You rest.'

For once she was glad to do as she was told. She watched wearily as he prepared their dinner. Every bone ached, but whether it was caused by the shock of her fall or the disappointment of their find, she wasn't sure. She

hadn't hurt herself in the fall, other than sustaining a
few bruises, so it must be the shock of finding the plane
which was making her feel so sick and defeated.

She was hardly aware of eating the food which Robb
placed in front of her. After a time, he took the plate
from her unresisting fingers and shook his head when he
saw how little she had eaten.

'I'm just not hungry,' she apologised.

'It's all right, I understand,' he assured her.

Depression and the strain of the day's activities had
combined to make her feel more tired than she had ever
been before. She must have dozed a little because she
came to with a start to find Robb reading some papers
which she recognised. They were from the old briefcase
he had found in the wreckage.

She struggled to sit up. 'Did you find anything
useful?'

He reacted with surprise as if he had thought her still
asleep. With a smooth motion, he refolded the papers
and slid them into his shirt pocket. 'Not really. Only old
business papers and flight plans.'

'But you're taking them back for the authorities?'

'Uh ... yes, I am.'

There was no need to be so coy about it, she thought
crossly. There was bound to be some sort of inquiry and
the Duncan name would be dragged through the mud
again. Since she couldn't go on defending her father
after today, it hardly seemed to matter any more. At least
her mother hadn't lived to see this day, which would
have broken her heart.

She stood up and stretched, needing the distraction of
some activity. Almost as a reflex action, she took her
notebook out of her rucksack and began to make notes

about finding the plane. She might never have the courage to write the story but the simple activity gave her fingers—and, more important, her mind—something to do.

She became aware that Robb was watching her intently. 'You really mean to write a story about this, don't you?'

Something in his tone made her wary. 'I might. Why?'

'I should have thought you, of all people, would want to let sleeping dogs lie.'

Did she have a choice? Once news of their find got out, the sleeping dogs would be well and truly awakened.

'I did come here on assignment, at my editor's expense,' she reminded Robb. 'He's going to expect results.'

'And you're going to give them to him, no matter who might get hurt?'

What did he mean? If anyone was hurt by the story, it would be Gemma herself. The reminder brought the tears welling into her eyes and she brushed them aside angrily.

'It's all very well for you,' she flung at him. 'You were right all along. My father did run away with the money that might have saved your property. Why don't you come out and say it?'

His hands balled into fists and she saw him relax them with an effort. 'Stop it, Gemma. I know you're angry, but taking it out on me won't change anything.'

Head flung back, she faced him defiantly. 'I'm not angry.'

'The hell you are! You have a right to be, knowing that your father let you think he was dead, when all the time he was living it up on someone else's money.'

Her control snapped. 'You bastard!' It might be true, but he had no right to say these terrible things to her. She launched herself at him, her fists flailing. But he caught and held her tightly against his muscular chest, letting her blows rain harmlessly against his back and shoulders.

It seemed to take for ever, but at last her anger spent itself and she rested her head against his shoulder. He didn't seem to mind that her tears were soaking into his shirt, and he resisted her feeble attempts to free herself.

She became aware that he was gently caressing her back and a shudder shook her, but this time it was a shudder of longing rather than unhappiness. She turned red-rimmed eyes to him. 'You goaded me on purpose, didn't you?'

'Maybe. After what you've been through today, you needed a safety valve.'

Embarrassed, she brushed the tears from his shirt. 'I'm sorry, I've made you all damp.'

His eyes slid over her face, feature by feature, and his smile was so warm that she felt a reflected heat building up inside her. 'There's no need to apologise. I'm glad there was something I could do to help.'

'Why would you want to?' she asked. 'After what we learned today, you have every right to despise me. My father did steal your money and make you lose your home. Now we've found the proof, I can't go on pretending to myself any longer.'

With a gentle gesture, he smoothed the tear-damp hair back from her face. 'You mustn't berate yourself, Gemma. Finding the plane only proved that your father survived the crash. We don't know enough to draw any more conclusions.'

Hope welled inside her like a living flame and she tilted her face up to his her eyes wide and moist. 'Then you don't hate me for reminding you of what you lost?'

His eyes darkened as if at a sudden inner pain but the look was quickly masked. 'I don't hate you, Gemma. If anything, you've helped to clear up a few things for me.'

Which still didn't make sense. 'I don't want your pity,' she said warningly.

'It isn't pity, damn it. I care about you.'

It was the last thing she had expected him to say. But nestled against him with her head resting against his chest, it was best to forget all the reasons why they were opposed and concentrate instead on how they could be friends.

As if sharing her thoughts, Robb's lips grazed the top of her head, sending shivers of sensation down her spine. As he pulled her close to him, she revelled in the hard, strong feel of his outdoorsman's body. Lifting her arms, she cupped her hands behind his neck and drew his head close to her face until mere inches separated them. 'Oh Robb,' she breathed. 'It shouldn't be like this, for us.'

He silenced her by claiming her mouth in a hungry kiss which told her she was not the only one who felt the strength of the attraction between them. His lips roved over her face and neck and when she closed her eyes to savour the sensation, he kissed her closed lids, elicting a gasp of response.

In turn, she shaped her hands to his back trying to draw him even closer to her. To steady them both, he propped a leg between her feet, the close contact leaving her in no doubt as to his feelings for her.

Inexorably, he urged her down on to the mossy grass and covered her body with his. One leg lay across her, making her a prisoner of his embrace. It was willing captivity, however, as she returned kiss for kiss, with a passion matching his. Tongues of fire travelled along her body and swirled around the pit of her stomach until she gave a cry of pure longing.

At this, he raised his head, his eyes alight with questions. But all he said was, 'Gemma?'

She knew what he was asking. She also knew she didn't want him to stop. Her senses reeling, she nodded.

It was all the invitation he needed. While he continued to make love to her with his eyes, he unfastened her shirt and his questing fingers found her swelling breasts. Her breathing quickened in response. Gradually, she allowed her eyes to close as she became lost in the kaleidoscope of delicious sensation his touch invoked.

Suddenly she sensed a change in him and she opened her eyes to regard him curiously. He had drawn back and lay beside her, propped on one elbow, his expression taut. 'Why did you stop?' she asked him, touching his face with a tentative hand.

He brushed her hand aside and pushed the edges of her shirt together. 'I don't want to do anything we might regret later.'

Her sense of confusion increased. 'What makes you think we would regret it?'

His fingers played up and down the curve of her hip, then as he realised what he was doing, he pulled the hand away. 'I'm not being fair to you, Gemma. There's a lot I haven't told you which might affect our relationship.'

He was being mysterious again, but she was damned if she would encourage it. 'I know enough to care about you. Surely that's all that matters?'

But instead of being pleased by her willingness to trust him, Robb seemed troubled by it. He uncoiled his considerable length from the grass and strode over to the campfire, where be began to rebuild the fading fire, giving the task all his attention. His back was to her, his shoulder stiff and set.

Why was he shutting her out like this? What was so wrong that he was unable to share it with her? She watched him for a few minutes, hoping he would offer her some sort of explanation. When none was forthcoming, she buttoned her shirt with shaking fingers. 'Robb, what is it?' she asked when she could bear his silence no longer.

'Nothing.'

She stared at him. 'Nothing? I must have done or said something which turned you off so suddenly. You might at least tell me what it was.'

He shook his head. 'No, you were the sensible one. It was my fault for thinking with my glands instead of my head. I'm sorry.'

She stared at him, feeling anger replace some of the hurt. 'You're sorry? For what?'

'For making love to you as if I had a right to.'

There it was again, that damned air of mystery. She felt it gather around them like a mist swirling in from the valleys. How she wished he wouldn't talk in riddles. If he had changed his mind about her because of what her father had done, at least he could be honest with her.

The mood was strained for the rest of the evening. They were polite enough as they attended to the chores and cleaned up the campsite, but Gemma was careful to unroll her sleeping-bag as far away from Robb's as she could. He had made her feel cheap, as if she let any man make love to her. In reality, it was very different. She was usually stand-offish to the point of prudery. Her journalist colleagues even teased her about it, saying she was letting the image down.

So Robb's remark about thinking with his glands instead of his head wounded her with its implication that she was the cause of his weakness. Well, she was damned if she would be accused of leading him astray a second time. She would be the original ice maiden from now on and see how he liked that!

She curled up in her sleeping-bag, trying to blot out her thoughts but they persisted. Kenneth Shelton had ended their engagement because she had a less-than-perfect pedigree. She had thought Robb was different but maybe, deep down, he felt the same way. Imagine having to go home and explain to his father that he was involved with a Duncan!

Her head was filled with the unpleasant possibility when she finally succumbed to sleep. But one thought was uppermost. Since she and Robb had to spend the rest of the trip in each other's company, she would be pleasant to him but that was all. She would carry off the rest of this trip with her pride intact. It was all she had left.

She awoke to the now-familiar smell of breakfast cooking but she choked on the thought of food. If only she could stay in her sleeping-bag all day, safe and warm, and not have to face Robb this morning.

She wasn't sure what had happened between them last night. They had been on the verge of a special closeness until he'd spoiled it with his cursed mysteries.

She stared up at the canopy of leaves overhead. What

if he had made love to her last night? She was still Jack
Duncan's daughter, and there was no way Robb's family
and friends would accept her, especially once news got
out that the plane wreck had been found with no cash on
board, and no sign of the pilot.

Maybe it was better this way.

She didn't really believe it, she found, as she washed
and dressed ready to face the day. She was attracted to
Robb Wetherill in a way that she could no longer deny.
No man had made her feel so special or cherished. Now
there was no hope of anything developing between
them, and the knowledge filled her with despair.

Despite her acceptance of the facts, her heart stirred
uncomfortably at the sight of Robb bending over the
campfire. He managed the blazing fire with an ease few
men could match. He looked totally at home in the bush,
a latter-day swagman of means.

He looked up and caught her staring at him. 'Good
morning. Is something the matter?'

'No, I was just watching you.' Confusion made the
colour rush to her cheeks and she looked away,
pretending interest in the view.

'I owe you an apology,' he said unexpectedly.

'There's no need . . .' she began but he forestalled her.

'Yes, there is. I shouldn't have taken advantage of you
the way I did. We were both overwrought and you were
especially vulnerable. It was all my fault.'

No, it wasn't, she thought guiltily. She had been as
ready as he was to melt into his arms and take the
comfort he was prepared to offer. If they had made love,
she would have been equally responsible. She remembered her vow to be dignified. 'You're right, it was a

trying day. We both got carried away. So let's forget it, shall we?'

He nodded agreement and she joined him at the campfire, accepting the plate of food he offered. As they ate in silence, she watched him covertly.

He seemed to regret his weakness last night, and expected her to feel the same way. But she didn't, not for a moment. It was true that she had been vulnerable when he approached her, but the only reason they hadn't made love was that Robb changed his mind. Had he forgotten that, or was he hoping she had?

It was later than they usually set off by the time they cleaned up their camp and buried the ashes of their fire. Gemma was surprised when Robb chose a path which would take them further into the mountain, instead of back down to the valley.

'Where are you going?'

'You want to find your father, don't you?' he asked in a strange tone.

She frowned. 'Of course I do. But you don't think he's still around here, do you?'

'Probably not. But his trail started from here, and I know someone who may be able to help us.'

Baffled, she followed him as he hiked deeper into the wilderness of the High Plains. Why was Robb looking for her father? What good would it do even if they found him? Unless he was determined to have his pound of flesh. She shivered at the prospect and wondered if she was still lying at the bottom of the gorge after her fall, hallucinating all this.

The camp they came upon at lunchtime was no hallucination, however. In a clearing stood two canvas tents, the old-fashioned kind held up by poles and guy-ropes. Beside them was a corral fashioned from timber poles and a number of brumbies paced restlessly inside it.

In the centre of the clearing was a square iron cookstand with billy-cans and misshapen saucepans standing on top. All was quiet.

'Whose camp is this?' she asked Robb in an undertone.

'It belongs to Jim Lovatt and his son Frank,' Robb explained. 'They make a living rounding up and breaking brumbies for the farmers, and hiring out as muster hands for the cattle drives.'

'Then they're out on the mountain now?'

'Probably.' He listened for a moment. 'Did you hear that?'

She strained to listen. Distantly, she heard a male voice calling what sounded like, 'Sa-a-alt!' She looked at Robb questioningly.

'They're broadcasting rock salt to attract the brumbies,' he supplied. 'In these mountains, centuries of rain and snow have leached the natural mineral salts out of the vegetation, so the animals who live here have a salt deficiency. The drovers carry saddlebags of salt which they broadcast over the open ground. The animals smell the stuff and come looking for it.'

'And can then be rounded up,' she finished for him. 'It's like something out of the last century.'

'People like Jim Lovatt live much the same as their forebears did,' Robb told her. 'But they wouldn't have it any other way. You ask Jim what he thinks of city life, when you meet him.'

She had a feeling she knew what the drover would say, and her conclusion was confirmed when he came riding into camp, leading a glistening-coated brumby which blew steam out of its nostrils, having given up the fight for freedom.

The man Robb hailed as Jim was a short, wiry man with not an ounce of spare flesh anywhere. He was all hard, compacted muscle and skin tanned to a deep mahogany. When he removed his stockman's hat, his hair was reduced to a few white strands, compensated for by a bushy beard sprinkled with grey. Deep furrows lined his eyes and nose, but his smile was open and friendly. 'G'day Robb, how's things?'

'Can't complain,' Robb said, falling into the other man's laconic way of speaking. 'How're you, Frank?'

'Real good, Robb,' the younger man said. In his late twenties, Frank was a younger version of his father, minus the beard, but with a thick moustache instead. Both men wore traditional mountain garb of moleskin trousers and Driza-Bone oilskin riding-coats.

Robb introduced her as Gemma Tate, a writer for *Outback* magazine. Tate, not Duncan, she noted wryly. She doubted whether the Lovatts, as friends of the Wetherills, would welcome a Duncan in their midst.

Jim insisted they should share the drovers' lunch of thick, meaty stew and dark-brewed billy tea. The simple food tasted delicious in the crisp mountain air, and they beamed with pleasure when Gemma said so.

'We don't often get city sheilas up here,' Frank said, earning a stern look from his father. 'Sorry, ladies.'

'It's all right,' Gemma smiled. 'I don't mind.'

'So what brings you to this out-of-the-way place?' Jim asked after the food and pleasantries were over.

'Gemma's writing a story about the disappearance of the *Plains Drifter*,' Robb explained, and she saw the men frown at the mention of the plane.

'We found the wreck yesterday,' Robb went on.

Jim pushed his hat far back on his head and scratched his forehead. 'You never?'

'They've been looking for that plane for five years,' Frank marvelled. 'Where did you find her?'

Robb told them, adding, 'The pilot may have survived. There was no trace of him in the wreckage, nor any sign that he was injured. I was hoping you blokes could tell us where he might have headed if he did walk away from the wreck.'

Jim shook his head. 'On foot, he wouldn't have had much of a chance up here.'

'He could have stumbled on one of the old-timers who live in these parts. They could have helped him,' Frank contributed.

Gemma recalled Robb telling her about the many eccentric characters who lived alone in the mountains, emerging as little as possible and only for essential supplies. 'Surely we would have heard something in that case,' she commented.

'Depends,' Jim said cryptically, 'on who he took up with.'

A tiny flame of hope flared in Gemma's heart but she refused to encourage it. 'Who would be most likely to take in a stranger up here?' she asked carefully.

'No question. Charlie Pines,' Jim said readily.

Robb, who had been silent, listening, up to now, smiled in recognition. 'Of course. Pines the Prospector. He could know something to help us at any rate.'

'I'm not saying he did, mind,' Jim cautioned. 'But he's such a crafty devil and so suspicious, he could do almost anything.'

'But if he's so suspicious, why would he take in a stranger?' Gemma asked.

'Depends. If the man was hurt, or needed help, he might consider it.'

Robb stood up. 'Where do we find Charlie Pines?'

Jim gave them the best directions he could, although they were necessarily vague. In the absence of signposts, they would have to rely on natural landmarks to locate the old prospector's hut.

They thanked Jim Lovatt and his son for their hospitality and left some of their own provisions in return. As they walked away, they heard the ringing cry of 'Sa-a-alt!' start up again behind them.

CHAPTER EIGHT

GEMMA'S heart hammered in her chest, but not with the effects of the altitude this time. What would they find when they reached Charlie Pines' cabin? Would he know anything about her father's whereabouts, or was it another false lead?

After all this time, she didn't dare to hope that her father could still be in the mountains. With the relief funds in his possession, he could have bought a new life for himself anywhere.

She studied Robb under quivering lashes. Didn't he understand what a trial this search was for her? He seemed oblivious to the turmoil raging inside her, as he ploughed doggedly ahead. Only her own determination to preserve what was left of her pride kept her following in his wake.

He certainly meant it when he said he finished what he started, she thought grimly. He seemed obsessed with tracking down Jack Duncan. What was unclear to her was why.

'Slow down, Robb,' she was forced to call as they started up a particularly steep bluff.

He looked back at her and slowed a little. 'Sorry. I forgot for a moment that I wasn't out here on my own.'

'Thanks a lot,' she said miserably.

'I didn't mean anything by it,' he rejoined, his tone sharp. 'We can take a rest if you like.'

'There's no need to stop on my account. I'd hate to come between you and your pound of flesh.' His stare was hard and cold, then he turned and pressed on without a word.

Charlie's hut turned out to be a rustic cabin of the type built by the early settlers in the mountains. Grey with age, it was built of local weatherboards and rusting iron, and stood on a rise, bordered on two sides by a fast-flowing creek.

Behind the main cabin was a wooden outbuilding, and in front stood the tumbledown remains of timber and scrub breaks, the holding yards built by stockmen to keep their sheep and cattle together at night.

The cabin was deserted, and there was no response to Robb's call.

She looked at him uncertainly. 'Could Charlie Pines be out on the mountain, like the Lovatts?'

'He could. We'll have to wait here and hope he comes back in a reasonable time.'

Suddenly the cabin door creaked open and a tall, spare man stood framed in the opening. He was gaunt and pale with a full beard and sparse grey hair standing out from his skull. He clung to the door frame for support. 'What do you want?'

No one else would have recognised him in his present condition, but Gemma did and a silent scream bubbled up in her throat. 'Dad?'

The man's eyes narrowed and he appraised her incuriously. 'Do I know you?'

A nightmarish sensation gripped her. 'It's me,

Gemma,' she whispered, forcing the words out through parched lips.

'Don't know you. Go away. Bloody tourists.'

Gemma reached for Robb and he put an arm around her shoulder. Gratefully, she leaned into the embrace. The man turned to go back into his cabin, but he swayed alarmingly. At once, Robb left her and went to his side.

Transfixed, Gemma stared at the two of them, her mouth stretched wide although no sound came out. Her father was alive. Alive! The word sang in her head. She wasn't the orphan she had supposed.

So why didn't he welcome her with open arms, instead of shutting her out? Anger boiled and bubbled inside her until she wanted to hit out at him and demand his recognition. He had no right to treat her like a stranger.

Unless . . . unless it was part of an act to justify what he had done. She remembered Robb's dire warning, 'He might not want to be found.'

But they *had* found him and she wasn't letting him go again, no matter what he did to her. She loved him. He had to love her back. He was her father.

'Gemma, for God's sake snap out of it. I need your help.'

Robb's commanding voice cut through her shock and she realised she was still staring at him, while he supported the swaying man. Like a sleep-walker, she moved towards them.

'What can I do?'

'Help me get him inside. He looks as if he's about to pass out on us.'

'What's the matter with him? He doesn't even know me.'

Awkwardly, with only one hand to spare, Robb reached across and gave her shoulder a rough jerk. 'Will you stop thinking about yourself? The man's ill. He needs your help, not you going to pieces.'

Hurt, both from Robb's touch and from his apparent insensitivity, combined to overcome her shock. 'I'm not entirely useless,' she said grimly. She fought the hysteria welling up inside her, and took the man's other arm as Robb directed. Together, they got the man into the cabin and settled into an armchair.

In shaky control once more, Gemma looked around the cabin, anything to keep her eyes from returning to the half-conscious man beside her.

The cabin was surprisingly light inside, the windows having been enlarged at some stage. The walls were of lath and plaster, covered with hessian for warmth. A fire had been laid in the brick fireplace and Robb set about getting it going.

'I'll be all right, there's no need to fuss,' the man insisted, regaining some of his senses.

Robb looked at him keenly. 'How long is it since you've eaten properly?'

The man shrugged. 'Can't remember. Charlie was due back with some supplies but he's a bit late. I couldn't go after him because of this blasted 'flu.'

So that was the reason for his dishevelled state. The man was ill and had no one to look after him. 'Something must have happened to Charlie or he would have returned by now,' Robb said grimly. He turned to Gemma. 'We'll have to do something. With no food for days and a dose of the 'flu, he could be in real danger.'

Panic threatened to overtake Gemma once more. To find her father now, only to lose him again to illness, was unthinkable. 'What are we going to do?' she asked Robb, her eyes wild with fear. 'What if we're too late and he dies? What if ...'

'That's enough!'

She could hardly believe he had struck her, even though her cheek stung from the impact and tears of pain sprang to her eyes. She clasped a hand to her stinging face and half turned away, but Robb turned her back to face him. 'I'm sorry, Gemma. I shouldn't have lashed out at you.'

She looked up at him, her face white but for the telltale red marks left by his fingers. He flinched when he saw them, and touched a gentle hand to the marks. She took a deep, steadying breath. 'I'll be all right,' she assured him shakily. 'It's just ... I never expected anything like this.' She spread her hands wide in a hopeless gesture.

'I know. And I wouldn't ask so much of you if I didn't think you were strong enough to handle it.'

With his words she felt some of her strength returning, although it was an effort to drag her eyes to the man half lying in the chair. But Robb was right. He needed her help right now. 'What do you want me to do?'

Under Robb's direction, she raided their rucksacks for dried soup and made it up with water, boiling it over the fire. There was some bacon in a meat-safe and she diced it, adding it to the soup to make it more nourishing. Then she spooned it into a thick china mug she found hanging from a hook over the sink.

With Robb's help, she persuaded the man to drink some of the soup and it revived him considerably. He settled back in the chair and fell into a light sleep. His breathing was already much easier than it had been when they found him.

'Do you think he'll be all right?' she asked, her voice vibrant with anxiety.

He nodded. 'If it was only lack of food added to the symptoms of the 'flu, he should recover completely after he's eaten a little more,' Robb observed. 'I think we got here just in time.' He looked at the sleeping figure. 'Are you sure it's him?'

'Do you think I wouldn't recognise my own father?' she flared up, then calmed herself. None of this was Robb's fault. 'Why is he like this? He doesn't even know me.'

Robb rested a hand on her shoulder. 'Calm down, Gemma. We don't have any of the facts yet. He seems to be suffering from some sort of amnesia.'

'Do you think it was caused by the crash?'

'It would explain why he stayed here so long,' Robb conceded.

'It would explain a lot of things. Oh Robb, if he really doesn't know who he is, that means he never intended to keep the money.'

'As I said, we don't know enough to draw any conclusions, so let's leave it for now.'

She contented herself with that, knowing he was right. 'What do you think happened to Charlie Pines?' she asked, changing the subject altogether.

Robb frowned. 'I don't know. He knew his friend was

depending on him, so he would have found his way back here if he could.'

'Unless he met with an accident,' she said, recalling her own brush with disaster. So many things could happen to someone alone in the mountains.

Robb stood up and reached for his jacket, and she shot him a curious glance. 'Where are you going?'

'To look for Charlie while it's still light. I'll get the Lovatts to help me.' His expression softened. 'You'll be all right here. He ... your father ... should sleep for some time. When he wakes up, you two will have plenty to talk about.'

All the same, she was disturbed by the idea of Robb going out on the mountain alone. He knew this region as well as any man alive but he wasn't immune to disaster. Charlie Pines was just as much at home in the High Country, yet where was he now?

'Don't look so worried, I'll try to get back before dark,' he assured her.

'It's not me, I ... was worried about you,' she confessed in a rush. 'Please take care.'

He gave her a long, curious look, his expression unfathomable. 'It's a novel sensation, having someone worry about me. But there's no need, I'll be fine.' He leaned forward as if about to drop a kiss on her forehead then apparently thought better of it and stroked her hair back with feather-light touch, then he let himself out and closed the door behind him.

Despite his assurances, she looked at the closed door with a feeling of trepidation. Lifting a hand to her forehead, she traced the mark of his touch, then dropped her hand self-consciously. She would have to stop this.

They had no chance of a future together so she would be foolish to encourage romantic notions about him.

Yet the feeling persisted. To dispel it, she turned to the man sleeping in the chair. Although the full beard obscured much of his features, his lined face was at rest, and there was no mistaking his identity. It was like a miracle, finding him alive and well after all this time.

Not quite well, she amended inwardly. Robb believed he had lost his memory in the crash, but it could be a symptom of the 'flu and his recent deprivation. Maybe he would know her when he awoke. It was a forlorn hope, but better than none.

To distract herself, she decided to clean and tidy the small dwelling. Although it was spartan, it was neatly kept, but, with her father ill and Charlie missing, the place hadn't been swept or dusted for a few days.

The work was satisfying, and the cabin looked much more homelike by the time she finished. Since her father still hadn't stirred, she took her dirty clothes out of her rucksack and washed them in the creek, hanging them to dry in the tree branches around the cabin.

After a moment's hesitation, she dug Robb's clothes out of his rucksack and washed them too. It was little enough to do for him, since he had refused to accept her money. And in doing it, she felt uncommonly like a wife. She was hanging out the last of his things, taking a ridiculous amount of pleasure in performing such an intimate task for him, when footsteps behind her startled her so she dropped the shirt she was holding.

'Robb,' she yelped. 'You scared the life out of me.'

'I'm sorry.' He picked up the shirt and looked at it in surprise. 'You didn't have to do this.'

'I wanted to,' she confessed, suddenly shy. Then she remembered his mission. 'Did you find out anything?'

'Soon after you and I left the Lovatts' camp, they stumbled on old Charlie Pines, lying injured in a gorge. He'd fallen trying to cross a creek. They think his leg is fractured.'

Her hand flew to her mouth. 'Will he be all right?'

Robb nodded. 'Frank Lovatt has taken him down the mountain for medical help. Jim was on his way up to tell us when I met him half-way.'

He paused, looking thoughtful. 'To set old Charlie's mind at rest, I told Jim to tell him that we would stay here with his friend until he's well enough to come back. It could be a few days.'

The idea of spending a few more days here with Robb was disquieting, and her uncertainty must have shown on her face because Robb said, 'I hope you don't mind me saying we would stay here.'

He couldn't know the reason for her uncertainty. 'My father is in there,' she reminded him. 'Of course I don't mind.'

The sound of someone moving around the cabin took them back inside. The man was awake and looked annoyed at their intrusion.

He mellowed a little when they explained what had happened to Charlie, but became suspicious when Robb said they had agreed to stay until Charlie returned. 'Why would you do that for me?'

Gemma dropped to her knees beside his chair and took his hand. 'You don't remember me, but I'm your daughter, Gemma. I want to stay and look after you.'

The man cleared his throat noisily and when he

looked at her his eyes were moist. 'Gemma, huh?'

She nodded and looked up at Robb, uncertain of what to do next. Robb came forward. 'Do you know who you are?'

The man looked embarrassed. 'I don't remember my real name. Charlie found me wandering in the bush so he called me the Happy Wanderer. Mostly he just calls me Happy. When I didn't get any better, he said I could stay with him.'

Robb and Gemma exchanged looks. 'When was this?' Robb asked.

'Four . . . no, five years ago now. That's right, Charlie and I have spent five Christmases together here.'

'And you've never left the mountain?'

'Charlie does all that.' He seemed about to say something else then thought better of it. 'What difference does it make anyway?'

'A lot, to me,' Gemma said gently.

Robb stood up and reached for his coat. 'I think that's my cue to take a walk outside. You two have family things to discuss.'

'Didn't you or Charlie realise that people would be looking for you, that you must belong somewhere, with people who care about you?' Her voice became husky and she broke off, unable to go on.

The man's hand tightened around hers. 'Yes, I thought of that. But I couldn't go back. You don't know what I've done or you wouldn't suggest it.'

If he remembered that he had done something wrong, then maybe the amnesia was an attempt by his mind to block the whole thing out, she thought with a sinking heart. People did that sometimes, when an event was too painful to remember.

'What do you think you did, Happy?' Robb asked, surprising her. She hadn't heard him come back in.

He held out a dirty canvas bag bearing the name of a large bank. It was the one whose offices had been used as collection points for the relief money.

Jack Duncan gave a groan of utter despair and covered his face with his hands. 'If you've found that then you must know I robbed a bank some years back.' He gave Gemma an agonised look. 'I'm on the run, that's why I can't go back.'

She stared at him, baffled. 'What?'

Robb came between them. 'That's why you've lived in the hills all this time, isn't it, Happy? And why Charlie has sheltered you here. You think this money came from a bank you robbed before you lost your memory?'

'Well, how else do you explain all that cash in the bank-bag being in my possession?' the man demanded.

Robb smiled broadly. 'There's a very good reason why you should have it.' He looked at Gemma. 'But I think your daughter ought to be the one to explain it.'

Haltingly, she told him about the relief fund and Jack's mercy flight to bring it to the stricken cattlemen. 'So you didn't steal it,' she assured him, hearing her own voice soar with gladness at the discovery. 'Your plane crashed in the mountains and you lost your memory.'

Jack Duncan stared at her in amazement. 'All this time I believed I must have robbed a bank. I was afraid to leave the mountain in case the police were looking for me to put me in jail.'

'Didn't Charlie mind when he thought you were a

bank-robber?' Robb asked curiously.

Jack Duncan grinned. 'He lost most of his money in the depression in the thirties. He doesn't have much time for banks, so he wasn't worried if I made off with some of their money. He thought it was justice if anything. Not that he ever touched a penny of the money. To him it was a great joke, having it here.'

He sobered suddenly. 'God, if only I'd known the truth. I wouldn't have had to hide up here wondering if every stranger had come to take me back.' He looked at Gemma with tragic eyes. 'What must you think of me, vanishing in such a fashion?'

'We didn't know what to think,' she answered truthfully. Her father had suffered enough, thinking he was a wanted man. There was no need to tell him about his family's anguish both at their loss and as the focus of suspicion.

'You don't know how happy you've made me, lass,' Jack Duncan said, ruffling her hair. 'I only wish I could remember you properly.' He twisted his head away. 'But I can't. You're a stranger to me, God help me.'

She squeezed his hand. 'It's all right, Dad. Don't distress yourself. Maybe having me here will help you to remember something.'

'I doubt it after all this time, but thanks anyway. I've tried and tried to remember, but it's as if there's a fog over my brain—like one of the mists we get up here. It covers everything, blanketing any sign or landmark so that I can't get past it, no matter how hard I try.'

'Then perhaps you shouldn't try,' she told him. 'You might do more harm than good.'

'But I want to remember. Especially now I know that

there's nothing in my past to run away from. I used to wonder if that was the reason why I couldn't remember anything. I'd wake up in the night, sweating, wondering if I'd maybe . . . killed someone.' His voice dropped to a whisper.

'Now stop that,' she instructed. 'You didn't harm anyone, so put it out of your mind.'

Jack smiled at Robb. 'She's a good girl, isn't she?'

'I think so,' Robb answered seriously.

Do you? her look asked him. But now wasn't the time to discuss his feelings. All the same, she wondered fleetingly what Robb thought of today's events. Her father was innocent. Her heart sang, but at the same time she knew Robb would take no comfort from the discovery. How could he when his father had led the crusade against the Duncan family?

She knew she should hold this fact against Robb, but her feelings for him kept getting in the way. Sneaking a glance at him was enough to set her pulses racing. No, she couldn't blame him. But could he forgive and forget so easily?

'Tell me about your mother,' Jack asked, interrupting her thoughts. 'My . . . my wife.' He said it haltingly, savouring the novel sound.

She wished she could be the bearer of better tidings. 'I'm afraid Mum died last year,' she said gently. 'But she never stopped loving you and hoping you would come back.'

A shadow crossed Jack Duncan's careworn features and he fingered his beard awkwardly. 'If she was anything like you, she must have been a terrific woman,' he said at last.

She looked away, embarrassed. 'She was a lovely person,' she said softly. 'After . . . after you disappeared, she worked very hard to keep us together as a family and make sure we had the best life possible.'

'Us?' Jack said at once. 'Are there other children then?'

'I have a younger brother, Tony—your son.'

'My son,' he echoed wistfully, pride in his voice. 'You wouldn't have any photos with you, I suppose.'

'As a matter of fact, I do.' She fished in her wallet and brought out two snapshots, a recent one of her and Tony by Lake Burley Griffin in Canberra, and an older photo of the whole family, taken just before Jack disappeared.

His eyes fastened on them hungrily. 'It *is* me,' he marvelled. 'And that must be your lovely mother. And— Tony, did you say?'

She nodded. It was odd discussing her family with him as if to a perfect stranger. To him, they were strangers, she realised. At his urging, she described their life in Canberra, her work as a journalist and Tony's newspaper cadetship. She was uncomfortably aware that Robb was absorbing every word as if he, too, wanted to know more about her background.

After a while, Jack slumped in his chair, obviously weary. He passed a hand over his eyes which were misty and red-rimmed. She tucked the photos into his shirt pocket and stood up. 'That's enough for now. You're still not over your 'flu, so why don't you lie down in the other room for a bit. Robb and I will be here if you need us.'

He did as bidden, shuffling into the other room with an unsteady gait which would have alarmed her if she hadn't shared his emotional unheaval. Finding him had affected her more deeply than she was letting Robb see.

Still, as if sensing her inner turmoil, he came back holding two tumblers of amber-coloured liquid. She took one and raised an eyebrow at him. 'What's this?'

'Brandy. These two may not keep much food in the house, but they had a couple of bottles of very good brandy in the back of a cupboard. I don't suppose Charlie will mind if we sample it.'

She took a steadying sip, then a deep breath. 'Robb, I'm sorry for the way I acted earlier. I'm not usually the hysterical type.'

'And I'm sorry I hit you. You were entitled to feel as you did. It must have been like seeing a ghost.' He poked at the fire, his expression thoughtful. 'You're also entitled to say "I told you so".'

'I thought that was your line.'

'But you believed in your father all along, while the rest of us thought the worst.'

She stared at the fire, losing herself in the flickering flames. It was an effort to rouse herself to speak. 'You weren't convinced of his guilt either, or you wouldn't have come on this expedition.'

'It's true,' he conceded, 'and I'm happy for you that it turned out for the best.'

Had it turned out so well, Gemma wondered? She had proved her father's innocence, but the gulf between her and Robb was wider than ever as a result. She closed her eyes against the pain of this thought. 'Where did you find the money?' she asked.

'In one of the outhouses behind the cabin. It wasn't even hidden. From the look of things, not a cent has been touched since it was packed.'

'Charlie must be very loyal, hiding my father here though they both believed he was a criminal,' she murmured.

Robb laughed. 'I think it was more than loyalty. Old Charlie enjoyed getting even with the banks for losing his savings in the depression. He must have a wicked sense of humour.'

'What will happen to the money now?'

He shrugged. 'It will probably go to charity the way the donors intended. The cattlemen have no need of it now, so it might be used to set up a fund for the next natural disaster.'

For some, it had come too late to make any difference, she thought unhappily. She took her notebook and pen out of her rucksack and sat down again.

Robb watched her curiously. 'What are you doing?'

'You're forgetting, I have a story to write.'

'Not now, surely?'

She thought he meant at the end of a tiring day. 'It's all right, I feel fine,' she assured him. 'I'm too keyed up to sleep anyway.'

'I didn't mean now in the time sense. I meant at all,' he stated.

She set her pen down. 'What are you trying to say, Robb?'

He spoke slowly and patiently, as if to a child. 'Writing that story won't change anything now. It may even do some harm. Your father doesn't remember anything of what happened, so writing the story won't help him.'

'I don't understand you, Robb Wetherill. I thought

you wanted the truth to come out.'

'Not if it means that someone will get hurt,' he continued.

'You don't mean Jack, surely?'

He leaned forward, his steady gaze meeting hers. 'Your father is happy up here. If you insist on writing his story, there'll be media all over this place, bothering him.'

Bothering Jack or bothering Robb, she wondered sourly. 'Why this sudden concern for my father's well-being?' she asked suspiciously. Was it a belated attack of conscience? Then the true reason hit her. 'It's your father and his precious friends you're worried about, isn't it? They won't look very good when it comes out that they persecuted an innocent family and jumped to some terribly wrong conclusions.'

He made a dismissive gesture with his hands. 'You don't know what you're talking about.'

'Don't I? You're not worried about my father or me, only your precious pride. Well, you know what you can do with it.'

Flinging her notebook down, she stalked outside into the gathering dusk, shivering as the crisp evening air hit her fire-warmed skin. Somewhere in the distance, an alpine dingo howled, setting her flesh creeping.

How could she ever have believed that Robb Wetherill cared for her?

All along, his only concern was to safeguard his own reputation and that of his precious cattlemen, she thought furiously. She wrapped her arms defensively around herself, both against the cold and the pain this idea brought with it. Robb didn't really care who got hurt as long as it wasn't one of his kind.

Unwillingly, she recalled the feel of Robb's arms around her and the warmth of his lips on her mouth. What a fraud he was, pretending that she meant something to him.

Some of her joy at finding her father had evaporated with Robb's unfeeling attitude. Couldn't he see that she wanted to tell the whole world that her father was not only alive, he was a hero—not the villain he had been painted. What was so wrong with that?

She imagined the cabin surrounded by TV crews and the pop of flashbulbs, and shuddered involuntarily. Robb might be right about keeping the media away. But she could still write the story without revealing the location of the cabin, surely?

She dismissed this idea out of hand. She knew better than anyone how tenacious a good reporter could be. They would find the place, no matter how carefully she disguised all reference to the location.

There was another way, though. It was obvious she wondered why she hadn't thought of it before.

Next morning while Robb was out fishing, she broached the idea to Jack Duncan. 'You can come to Canberra and live with me. Even though you don't remember us, Tony and I would love to have you near us. We might even find a doctor who can help you.'

Her voice vibrated with hope but Jack Duncan shook his head regretfully. 'I'm an old man, Gemma. No,' he held up his hand when she opened her mouth to protest. 'Don't argue, dear. I've spent the last five years living up here with nobody but Charlie and the animals for

company. I couldn't handle city life any more, especially
not the way I am now. Imagine how I'd feel if someone
greeted me in the street and I didn't know who they
were.'

'I could coach you and help you,' she offered.

He rumpled her hair affectionately, unaware that the
gesture brought tears to her eyes. He didn't remember,
as she did, how he had done the same thing when she was
a little girl. 'I know you'd do everything you could for
me, and I'm more grateful than I can say. But you have
your own life to live, just as I have mine. With no past,
I'm better off here.'

She surveyed the sparsely furnished cabin with its
sagging armchairs and hessian-lined walls. From them
hung the stock-whips, halters and ropes which Jack had
told her Charlie made from greenhide leather he tanned
himself. Selling the artefacts on his rare visits to town
gave him a small income to buy supplies.

'But you have so little here,' she said worriedly. 'You
nearly died because you were ill and there was nobody
around to help you. What if it happened again?'

'If it happens, it happens,' Jack said philosophically.
'I'd be no loss to anybody.'

A pang shot through her and she shook her head,
feeling her eyes brim with tears. 'You would be to me.'

He laughed for the first time in ages and she was glad
to see that some of his pallor had gone. Good food and a
little nursing care had done wonders for him. 'It
gladdens my heart to hear you say it,' he confessed. 'But
it doesn't alter the fact that I'm happy here. I'd love you
and your brother to keep in touch with me, even though
I don't remember either of you. But you should return

home with your boyfriend. He's a terrific bloke and just right for you, from what I've seen of him.'

She tensed, wondering what he had seen to reach such a conclusion. Was she betraying her attraction to Robb in ways she hadn't been aware of doing? 'Robb isn't my boyfriend,' she said a little stiffly.

Jack Duncan's eyes twinkled. 'Then he ought to be. I've seen the ways he looks at you. That man is head over heels in love with you, take my word for it.'

'Rubbish,' she said, discomfited. 'He's only here to protect his own interests.'

Jack sighed as if at her lack of perception. 'Have you ever considered that the most important of those interests could be you?'

CHAPTER NINE

ALTHOUGH Gemma had dismissed Jack's notion that Robb's interest in her was personal, the thought lingered. In the next few days, she found herself paying careful attention to Robb.

He was no more nor less solicitous than he had been since they left Omeo. It was only when he thought she wasn't looking at him that his expression changed, becoming dreamlike, as if she was in his thoughts in some special way.

What a ridiculous idea! She was annoyed with herself for letting Jack plant it in her head. To Robb, she was only a colossal nuisance who refused to let sleeping dogs lie.

He didn't know it, but she still hadn't made up her mind whether or not to write her story. It would clear her father's name—and her own, she acknowledged. Was that why she was so keen to do it? But it would also expose Jack to unwelcome publicity, bringing outsiders prying into his life—a life he insisted suited him, despite its shortcomings. Ought Gemma to put his preferences before her pride?

In desperation, she pushed the question to the back of her mind and concentrated on enjoying her stay at Charlie's cabin.

She could worry about what to tell the world when they rejoined it in a few days' time.

Meanwhile, she resolved to make the most of the mountain solitude and beauty. It was unlike anywhere she had been before. Never having strayed this far outside civilisation before, she was surprised to find herself enjoying it so wholeheartedly.

Even the lack of newspapers, radio and television ceased to bother her after a day or so of missing them. The outside world with all its cares might have ceased to exist.

'Enjoying yourself?' Jack Duncan asked when he joined her on the rough-hewn veranda one afternoon.

'I'm thriving on all this mountain air.' She looked up at him with a rush of affection. Having her father back after believing for so long that he was dead was like a miracle.

Side by side, they leaned against the split rails edging the veranda, and surveyed the lushness of Charlie's alpine hideaway. It was so ruggedly beautiful that Gemma felt moved almost to tears.

At this altitude, the snow gums were twisted into bizarre shapes where they had been ravaged by gales or overloaded with snow. The air was fragrant with the sweet scent of aromatic plants and grasses which grew nowhere but here.

Overhead, kestrels wheeled and called, and swallows swooped and dived above the creek, looking for moths and other insects.

Gemma had never seen so many birds before, from the cockatoos known locally as cocky johns to the flocks of wild ducks which V-planed across the sky to their favourite watering holes each evening.

The plant life was also varied and spectacular, from

the stumpy black boys with their punk haircuts of green fronds to the emerald foliage of the sub-tropical trees along the creeks and gullies.

'I could never get tired of looking at all this,' she sighed to the silent man alongside her.

'Now you know why I don't want to leave it,' he said. 'Can you honestly tell me that your city has more peace and joy to offer than all this?'

She shook her head. 'I'm afraid not.' She had avoided telling him about the heartache he had endured when he had had to leave his job in Canberra. As far as he knew, he had never done anything else but pilot chartered planes. She couldn't see any point in spoiling an illusion which made him happy and hurt no one.

When she described how he used to run the charter service out of Omeo his face took on a luminous, wistful quality as if he longed to remember that part and regretted that he was unable to recall it.

They talked as well about Gemma's family. Jack was hungry for details, as if they could replace the memories he had lost. 'I must arrange for Tony to visit you here,' she said impulsively.

'Do you think he'd come?'

'Why shouldn't he?'

'Well, he might be embarrassed at finding me . . . like this.'

'There's nothing wrong with the way you are,' she assured him. His uncertainty had surfaced before and she was only now beginning to convince him that she didn't blame him for what had happened. 'None of it was your fault,' she repeated yet again. 'Tony will understand, so stop worrying. He's a lot like you, in many ways.'

Jack's eyes shone. 'Is he?'

'Not to look at, but in character. He's a bit shy and lacking in self-assurance, but clever and gentle.'

Jack Duncan laughed. 'I'm not sure that's a compliment. You make me sound like a real softy.'

She rested her head on his shoulder. 'You are a softy. At least you always were where I was concerned.'

His arm came around her for a moment. 'I'll have to take your word for it, but I can see why it's possible. With a daughter like you, who could be stern and tough?'

Not you, she remembered dreamily. He had tried to be firm but she had usually got her own way in the end. Maybe it wasn't good for her, but his indulgence had been something to look back on with pleasure when times became harder.

'Are you sure you won't come and live with me?' she tried again. 'You don't have to live in town. We could rent a farm around Queenbeyan, and I could commute to work each day.'

'I'm sorry,' he said, sounding genuinely regretful. 'It will be hard giving you up when it's time for you to leave, but I'd have to sooner or later, even if I moved in with you. What about when you get married? You won't want your old man hanging around then.'

Your old man. How wonderful it sounded, reminding her that she really did have a father again. 'I wouldn't worry about my getting married,' she laughed. 'There's no one in the offing as yet.'

'Wasn't there a bloke in Canberra?' her father asked.

'You mentioned his name. A politician or something.'

'Kenneth Shelton,' she supplied. 'He's a journalist on my magazine, but he wants to be a politician. It's over between us now.'

'No regrets?'

She thought for a moment. 'Perhaps a few. We were together for quite some time. But I could never meet his standards for a wife.' She didn't tell him the main reason why Kenneth had broken off their relationship. Jack would hate to be the cause of any unhappiness for her, and she wasn't sure that she herself was all that unhappy about it.

Kenneth seemed far away now. It was hard even to remember what he looked like. Every time she tried to recall his features they were replaced by a strong, angular face with an uneven nose, remote gold-flecked eyes and close-cropped hair the colour of a dingo's pelt.

'What about young Wetherill?' her father asked, interrupting her reverie.

She stared, wondering whether she had betrayed herself. 'Robb and I are just friends,' she said emphatically.

'Friendship is a good place to start, I suppose,' Jack speculated.

'Now stop it,' she half teased. 'I don't need a matchmaker, even if he is my father.'

Jack rumpled her hair in the now-familiar gesture. 'You're a funny girl, so city-smart in some ways. But you can't see what's right under your nose.'

'And you can, I suppose?'

'Remember, my brain isn't cluttered with the past. I have nothing to do but think about the present and the future,' he told her. 'In Robb Wetherill, I see a man who cares deeply about you, but holds back because he isn't sure how you feel about him.'

'Maybe that's because I don't know how I feel myself yet,' she blurted out.

'What's wrong with telling him that much, then?'

Leaving the question hanging in the air, Jack went back inside for the afternoon nap which had become a habit since Robb and Gemma had arrived. He was fully recovered from his 'flu now, but still seemed to need the extra rest. Whether it was for this reason alone, or to give Robb and Gemma a chance to be by themselves, she wasn't sure.

Soon afterwards, she heard Robb whistling as he climbed the slope to the cabin. From a metal ring over his shoulder hung a pair of fat brown trout which would provide their evening meal. 'Is Jack asleep?' he asked as he joined her on the veranda and prepared to clean the fish.

'He just went in,' he rejoined. Jack's comments about Robb had made her uncomfortable in his presence. Jack couldn't be right about the way Robb felt. There was so much hostility between them still. For one thing, Robb was still opposed to her plan to write Jack's story.

'You love it up here, don't you?' she asked Robb, surprising herself. She hadn't meant to say any such thing.

He looked up and nodded. 'If it was practical, I'd do what Charlie and Jack do and live here all the year round.'

'But you need to earn a living,' she guessed.

'It's not only the money. One can survive on very little

up here. Charlie makes enough from his leather goods to get by. I guess I'd miss the amenities of town life, if I'm honest.' He looked up quickly. 'Not that I could ever live in a city or town, but I like to have one near by.'

'The best of both worlds,' she intoned softly.

He regarded her with surprise. 'I didn't really think you'd understand.'

'I told you I love the mountains,' she said irritably. 'Why is it so hard to believe me?'

'Maybe because I've heard it before,' he said, giving all his attention to the fish.

Now was her chance to ask the question which had been on her mind since they located the wreck. 'Was it a woman who told you that?'

'How did you know?'

'I got the feeling there had been someone ... important to you, who had hurt you in some way. Was she a city girl?'

'Her name was Allison,' he explained in a voice barely above a whisper. 'We grew up together in Omeo and it was taken for granted that we'd marry.'

'What happened?'

'During the ski season, she was swept off her feet by a banker from Melbourne.'

'But if you had an understanding ...'

'Apparently her understanding was different from mine,' he interjected harshly. 'On the night of what was supposedly our engagement party, she disappeared, leaving a note to say she'd gone to join this man. I never heard from her again.'

She felt a surge of compassion for him. 'What a terrible way to find out. Were you in love with her?'

He shrugged. 'I thought I was. Now, with hindsight, I'm not sure if it was love or habit which kept us together. But it was enough to make me realise I couldn't compete with the bright lights and life in the fast lane.'

At least she understood his aversion to city people. 'It doesn't mean everyone from the city is the same,' she said defensively. 'You were just unlucky.'

'Twice?' he queried.

She looked at him, startled. 'It happened again?'

'She was a ski-instructor I worked with at Mount Hotham. We started seeing a lot of each other and it looked like lasting, then . . . you guessed it.'

'She left for the city?'

'Give the lady a cigar.' His voice was bitter. 'This time there wasn't even a man as her excuse. She told me she didn't want to spend her life stuck out in the sticks.'

'Oh Robb, I'm sorry.' Her voice was vibrant with sympathy.

'You needn't feel sorry for me. I learned my lesson.' He picked up the fish and opened the fly-screen door. 'I'll call you when dinner's ready.'

Before she could offer to do the cooking, he went inside, leaving her alone with her thoughts.

Poor Robb. Imagine being hurt not once, but twice, and both times in the same way. No wonder he wasn't prepared to trust his heart to a city girl a third time.

She sighed heavily. He was attracted to her, she knew it now. And she accepted that she felt the same way. But she had no hope of convincing him that she loved the same things as he did. The longer she stayed in the mountains, the less the city called to her. How could she make Robb believe her?

A slow smile spread across her even features as she considered the most obvious way to convince him. It was worth a try!

She said nothing about her plans for the remainder of their stay. She didn't want to take a chance on Robb talking her out of her course of action.

So anxious was she to make a start that she was relieved when Jim Lovatt rode in and told them that Charlie Pines was being released from hospital the next day.

'Does that mean we can leave here?' she asked, her eyes shining with anticipation.

'I guess so,' Jim concurred. 'Frank and I are handy if Jack needs anything before Charlie gets back.'

They had explained to Jim Lovatt who Jack Duncan was. He would never be known as the anonymous Happy ever again. 'I can take care of myself. I don't need a nursemaid,' he grumbled when he heard Jim's comment.

'Now you're over your 'flu, of course not,' Gemma agreed. 'But I'll have an easier mind knowing you have friends on call up here.'

Robb looked at her darkly. 'Are you really so keen to get away?'

She was but not for the reason he must be thinking. She felt no urgency to be away from him, the opposite in fact. 'I'm ready to go,' she said unhelpfully. 'My clothes are sticking to me. I only brought enough for a few days, not for a couple of weeks of mountain living.' Even though she had been able to launder her clothes regularly, they were stiff and uncomfortable from the rough soap and hard water at Charlie's cabin.

'I see. Then we won't hang around,' Robb said stiffly.

She wished she could reassure him, but there would be time enough later. For now, she wanted to get back down the mountain as quickly as possible and put her plan into action.

There was one more thing she wanted to do, however.

'Can we take a last look at the plane-wreck before we go down?' she asked Robb.

'If you like,' he agreed readily. Since she made it clear that she was eager to get away, he had been quiet and withdrawn, as if her attitude bothered him.

'Are you sure you'll be all right until Charlie gets back?' she asked her father for the umpteenth time.

He professed annoyance. 'Stop worrying, girlie. I've had all I can take of female chatter and I'll be glad to see the back of you.' Even as he said it, she knew it wasn't true. There was a definite brightness in his eyes and he kept rubbing them with the back of his hand as if they bothered him. Strangely enough, her eyes were bothering her too.

'I'll be back,' she promised as they shouldered their gear for the downward trek.

'Not too soon,' he said gruffly. His face said the opposite.

He watched them until they were almost out of sight, then turned back towards the cabin, a gaunt, solitary figure.

'I don't like leaving him alone up there,' she said to Robb as they hiked deeper into the forest.

He didn't remind her of how eager she had been to

leave a while ago, but he was probably thinking it.

'He'll be fine. Jim and Frank Lovatt have promised to call by regularly. And Charlie will be back tomorrow.'

'But he'll be on crutches. How will he get around the mountain with a broken leg?'

'Mountain men are a special breed,' he told her. 'They're more resilient than average. They must be to survive up here.'

A special breed, she thought, surveying him covertly from under lowered lashes. Yes, Robb Wetherill, you are definitely that.

'There's one thing puzzling me,' she said as they walked. 'Wouldn't Charlie hear about the plane crash, and guess where my father came from?'

'Sometimes I think the world could come to an end and these people wouldn't know it,' Robb observed. 'With no television, no radio and no newspapers, they're completely cut off. You couldn't even land a helicopter near them with all that dense tree cover.'

'What about the bush telegraph?'

'It does operate, even up here. But not with eccentrics like Charlie Pines. He keeps himself to himself and expects everyone else to do the same. The wonder is that he ever agreed to take Jack Duncan into his home in the first place.'

She had a sudden flash of insight. 'Does Charlie Pines collect stray animals?'

Robb looked at her curiously. 'As it happens, he does. There's usually a sick possum or abandoned baby kangaroo in his care, although I didn't see any this time.'

'I did,' she said triumphantly. 'Jack pointed out a kestrel with a damaged wing. It was recuperating in a tree near the cabin. That explains it.'

He was still mystified. 'Explains what?'

'Charlie's response to Jack's need. He was a sick animal, in need of care. If Dad had been healthy and whole, Charlie would probably have chased him away.'

'You know, I think you're right,' he agreed. 'But I'm not sure your father would like being described as a sick animal.'

'Why not? It's how he thinks of himself.'

Robb made no comment but he must have noticed Jack's total lack of self-confidence. Maybe it came with losing your memory and all sense of your own identity. It was hard to imagine how that must feel. No wonder he felt safer staying in the sheltering mountains, away from the demands of civilisation.

They hiked along in silence for a while, the downhill trek proving much easier than the climb up had been. Gemma still needed to watch her step. One slip could send her careering down the mountain, a terrifying experience she had no wish to repeat.

At lunchtime, they passed the Lovatts' camp, which was deserted. Although they listened, there was no ringing cry of 'Salt' to indicate that the brumby hunters were nearby.

'They could have gone to the hospital to see Charlie,' Robb speculated. 'We can borrow their camp for a short time and leave them some fish in return.'

Gemma eyed her trout sandwiches with distaste. 'A week of mostly fish meals has turned me into a rabid carnivore,' she swore. 'I can't wait to get back to a juicy grilled steak.'

'I know the feeling,' Robb grinned. 'But without the

fish, our provisions wouldn't have lasted the distance.'
They wouldn't even have stretched this far but for some
fresh supplies brought to them by the Lovatts during
their enforced stay at the cabin. They had left Omeo
prepared for only a few days of bushwalking, not the ten
days this expedition had turned into. Her editor must be
wondering what had become of her.

'What are you thinking about?' Robb asked, noting
her pensive expression.

'My editor,' she said without thinking. 'I haven't
been in touch for over a week. He'll wonder what's
happened to me.'

'And to his story,' Robb said sourly. 'You're still
determined to write it, I suppose.'

'I don't know,' she answered truthfully. 'At first it
seemed like a good idea. Now, I'm not so sure.'

'Well, that's something, at least.'

Her confession seemed to brighten his mood and he
trod with a light step down the mountain. Just when she
was wondering whether they would be able to locate the
plane-wreck again, he led her to the edge of a steep gully.

'There she is.'

She peered over the edge, recognising the place.
Below them, a trail of broken branches and skid-marks
traced her fall. She shuddered. There had to be an easier
way down.

Robb found it with his usual efficiency. Using sturdy
tree-trunks and tussocks of grass for hand-holds, he
climbed down to the wreck which was still shrouded in
greenery. How had he ever spotted it from above?

'Careful now. There's a foothold just to your left,' he
instructed, guiding her down. Suddenly his hands

spanned her waist and he lifted her the last few feet to the floor of the gorge. It was a warm day and their walk had heated them both up. Even so, his hands felt fiery through her shirt.

When he left his hands around her, she looked up at him, flustered. 'What is it?' Then she knew. He meant to kiss her. Here. Now.

His eyes were warm and caressing. 'Gemma?'

'Yes.' It was a question and an answer all at once.

He needed no more encouragement. His hands skimmed from her waist to her shoulders and he pulled her against him.

Instantly she knew it was where she belonged. They hadn't spent more than snatches of time alone since they had arrived at Charlie's cabin. Now she recognised that the ache she felt was for Robb's touch. For as soon as he took her in his arms, the hollow sensation subsided.

In its place she felt breathless, as if her heart had lodged in her throat and was constricting her breathing. Her hands, which she had instinctively placed against his chest, slid up around his neck.

He fumbled behind her and released the rucksack she still carried, letting it drop on to the mossy ground. Then he clasped his hands around her shoulders and pressed his mouth hard against hers.

She felt dizzy as his kiss triggered a yearning deep inside her, demanding release. She found none in Robb's embrace which banked the flames of desire ever higher within her.

'Oh, Robb,' she moaned, hearing her own voice throaty with desire as his kiss plumbed the depths of her soul.

'Gemma.' He made her name sound like an invitation. 'I wanted to do this days ago, but your father was always around.'

So she was right about the tender glances he kept giving her. 'I know,' she soothed. 'I felt it too.'

'I was sure you did, but you never showed it.'

Her hands twined in the tawny hair at the nape of his neck and he shivered with pleasure. 'I told myself I was imagining things.'

He kissed her again. 'This isn't imagination.' And again. 'Or this.'

Much more and she would melt into a stream of pure desire, she thought desperately. She freed her mouth by ducking her head so that his kisses rained on to her forehead and hairline, giving herself time to think. But with her face buried against his chest, she was even more distracted by the male scent of him which was playing havoc with her hormones. 'But attraction is one thing. Love is another.'

'And which is this?' he murmured against her hair.

'I'd like to think it's love. But how can it be when we know so little about each other and the past keeps getting in our way?'

'Not any more,' he reminded her. 'As for the first objection, how much better can you know someone than after spending a week in the wilderness with them?'

He had a point. 'But there's still the problem of the story I want to write.'

'Forget the story,' he insisted.

She struggled to free herself enough to face him. 'I can't forget it. How else can I restore Dad's good name?'

'And incriminate mine,' he threw at her.

'It isn't as bad as that. I know the cattlemen who pilloried my mother won't like being held accountable for their actions but I can't help it. They didn't stop to worry about my family's feelings.'

Robb raked a hand through his hair. 'You can't do it, Gemma. If you write that story, you destroy any chance of a future for us.'

'But why?'

He took a deep, shuddering breath. 'Isn't is enough that I'm asking you not to write it?'

Tears of frustration stung her eyes. 'No, it isn't.' His touch had inflamed her to fever-pitch, leaving her a quivering mass of unfulfilled longings. She wasn't up to this conversation right now. Not when every fibre of her being longed to be held and caressed and ... yes, made love to.

'I don't understand you, Robb Wetherill,' she breathed, feeling her breasts chafing against her shirt, their nipples sensitised by his embrace. What right did he have to arouse her like this then break it off just because she stood by her principles?

Suddenly, she understood his motives. 'So that's it,' she snarled, frustration and humiliation threatening to rob her of her voice. 'You thought if you made love to me I'd meekly give in to your wishes, didn't you? You don't care what tactics you use as long as you get your own way.'

'Stop it, Gemma,' he commanded. 'You've got it all wrong.'

No, she hadn't. He was as transparent as glass. 'All that talk about wanting me and wishing we were alone at the cabin was the warm-up,' she persisted. 'You thought you only had to convince me you cared for me and I'd go along with whatever you wanted, including scrapping the story. What came next—declarations of love?'

He looked genuinely distressed. 'Don't, Gemma. Damn it, I do care about you!'

'Then prove it. In fairness to my father, let me write his story, and we'll go on from there.'

'Very well, write your damned story,' he rasped in a voice which was hoarse with pain. 'But we won't go on from there. Enjoy your moment of journalistic triumph, because I won't be here when you come back.'

CHAPTER TEN

SHE shook her head to rid it of the confusion which clouded her brain. 'What do you mean, you won't be here?'

There was a long, anguished silence, then he seemed to collapse inwardly like a pricked balloon. 'All right, I'll make it as plain as I can. The briefcase I found in the wreck contained more than flight plans. The papers showed who was to receive the relief funds. The owner of Wyuna was listed, but it wasn't my father.'

'I'm not sure I understand. How could anyone else be the owner of Wyuna at that time?'

'My father is a compulsive gambler. That's his particular weakness. The documents in the briefcase prove that it wasn't the bushfire which prevented my father from holding on to Wyuna. It was already gone before the fires even started. Either he gambled it away or used it as security for his debts, it hardly matters now. The point is, the new owner was the one who would have received the relief money, not my father.'

'Oh, my God!'

It was the last thing she had expected to hear. Now she understood why Robb didn't want her to write about finding the wreck. It could spark a string of background stories, any one of which might make Wyuna's real fate public, destroying Mick Wetherill's standing in the area. 'Why did your father pretend that he was forced to sell because of the fire?' she asked, stunned.

'He was so ashamed of what he'd done, he couldn't bring himself to tell anyone, even me. The disappearance of the money provided the perfect cover story.'

'So he let another man take the blame for his losses, ruining the reputation of innocent people to save his own,' she blazed as she added it up.

'Please don't,' Robb said, his voice cracking with emotion. 'It doesn't change anything now. Can't you find it in your heart to feel sorry for a broken old man?'

'The way he felt sorry for my mother and brother?' she asked acidly. 'I'm not sure I'm that big a person, Robb. How long have you known the truth?'

'I suspected it before we set off from Omeo, after I went to see my father to ask him about the search. He was evasive and contradicted himself on the details, making me wonder what he was hiding. I knew he had a weakness for gambling, so I guessed the rest.'

'So that's why you were so keen to come with me. You said you had your reasons.'

He reached out to her but she shrank away, not wanting her physical needs to cloud her judgement. Whatever stood between them, she was still desperately vulnerable to his touch. 'How could you?' she cried, despair making her voice shrill. 'How could you make love to me, knowing that it was all a lie?' This was the hardest thing to accept.

His eyes blazed. 'That part wasn't a lie, I swear. Despite my experiences with city girls, you got under my skin and stayed there, no matter how hard I tried to dislodge you. I kept telling myself you'd be off back to the bright lights once this trip was over. But nothing mattered except how much I wanted you in my arms.'

She wanted to believe him, but how could she, when she knew he was using her to protect his good name? In a small community like his, he would suffer as badly as his father if the truth came out. Her mother had discovered that the hard way.

She turned away, tensing as she heard him start to follow her. She quickened her steps wanting to put some distance between them, then cried out in pain as her ankle caught in the twisted root of an alpine ash growing out of the side of the hillside. She fell heavily, drawing a sharp breath as pain knifed through her ankle.

Anger welled up inside her, at him and at her own stupidity. To hurt herself now, after surviving all that Robb and the elements could do to her, was too much. She slid her boot zipper down and massaged the ankle which was throbbing fiercely.

Instantly, Robb was on his knees beside her, his sensitive fingers probing the extent of her injury. 'You've twisted it badly, but I don't think it's broken.'

He helped her to stand and she was relieved to find she could—just. 'We'll take it slowly going back,' he promised. 'If necessary, I can carry you.'

'I'll walk, thanks,' she said through gritted teeth. The last thing she needed was to find herself in his arms, creating even more havoc with her senses.

With her ankle bound up and a crutch cut from a dead tree to support her, she made it back to Joe McCabe's house where they retrieved the horses. The length of time they had been away must have raised

Joe's eyebrows, but he made no comments as he helped them to saddle up.

Once on horseback, their progress was faster. Her ankle was still sore but much improved by the time they reached Robb's house. The sight of it confused her. She ought to be glad the trip was almost over, yet she found herself regretting the imminent parting more than she would have believed possible.

'My car will be waiting when I get back,' she said.

'For all the good it will do you. You can't drive anywhere until your ankle heals.'

Damn her clumsiness in falling so close to the end of the trip! Robb seemed quite happy to have her as a house-guest again, but, knowing she was to spend still more time in his company, she didn't know whether she was glad or sorry.

All she could think about was the way Robb had used her feelings for him to try to change her mind about writing the story. She understood his trepidation. Once the truth about her father's disappearance came out, it wouldn't be long before someone discovered that Wyuna had changed hands before the bushfire, not afterwards as was now believed.

To Robb's father, the whole thing had been a godsend, giving him the perfect excuse to sell Wyuna. He must have gone through hell wondering if the wreck would be discovered and he would be found out. Unless . . . no, it was too awful to think he might have deliberately led the search astray to protect himself. She couldn't believe such a thing of anyone with a spark of human decency.

All the same, she had to know. 'Robb, you don't

think your father found the wreck and kept quiet to avoid discovery, do you?' she asked him that evening as they relaxed in the living-room, enjoying amenities like chairs and electric light again.

The explosion she half expected never came. 'I considered the possibility,' he said grimly. 'My God, if I believed he did, I'd turn him in myself. But if he had stumbled on the wreck, he could have destroyed the papers which proved that he lied. With the money still missing, the end result would have been the same. So there's no way he could have located the wreck.'

'Are you going to tell him what we found?'

He spoke from behind the hand covering his eyes. 'God knows. I'm still thinking it over.'

'Does it change how you feel about your father?'

His eyes narrowed as his gaze met hers then flickered away. 'You were still loyal to Jack, no matter what he was supposed to have done. I guess it's true about blood being thicker than water.'

'But you were devastated by the loss of your property.'

'Mainly because I thought it had been stolen from us. Now I know we lost it because of Dad's weakness, I feel differently. I even understand why my mother left home when I was young. It wasn't the lure of the city, as I'd always thought. She couldn't take any more of Dad's gambling. So it's helped me to understand a lot of things about my life. And the property was Dad's to lose. I should never have planned my life around my expectations.'

He was being too hard on himself. 'It was a reasonable expectation.'

'Maybe, maybe not. But it made me build a life of my own. Who knows, I may buy my own cattle station one day. A few more skiing championships ought to make it possible. So I can't see what good it will do letting Dad know I've found out his secret.'

'Unless it relieves his mind,' she suggested. 'It can't be easy living with a lie like his.'

He turned accusing eyes on her. 'Or unless you still intend to write about it now you know the harm you would be doing.'

'I told you, I haven't made up my mind yet,' Why did he keep harping on the same question? 'I may not have any choice if my editor insists on a story. He sent me down here, remember?'

'What would he have done if we'd found nothing?'

'How should I know?' she almost shouted. 'It's beside the point, since we did find something.'

She was sitting on the couch with her injured ankle propped up on a cushion, and he came and knelt beside her. 'Can't we forget the plane for a while? I found something much more important to me on that mountain, and I think you did, too, only you won't admit it to yourself.'

There was a sudden tension in the air as if it had become charged with electricity, and she found herself leaning towards Robb as if pulled on an invisible string.

He leaned towards her and their lips met, sweeping aside everything else. His hand moved up the curve of her thigh and slid inside the embroidered silk shirt she had donned earlier. There was nothing underneath it and she felt his hand, hot and caressing, as it slid over her skin.

She gasped as he found the swelling curve of her breasts, and massaged each in turn to pert, expectant life. Her arm which was loosely draped around his shoulder pulled him closer as she sought his mouth.

Hers was open and ready and he invaded it willingly, plundering her tender palate with his tongue, until her whole being pulsated with longing for him.

Rising to his knees, he took her in his arms so that he could kiss her more thoroughly while their bodies touched intimately.

With a fevered groan, he slid on to the couch beside her, stretching full length in the confined space so that they lay thigh to thigh.

This was insane, she told herself wildly. If she let him make love to her now, she would be betraying not only herself, but her family as well. What was she doing, entwined in Robb's arms when she knew it must end soon?

At the same time, her body silenced her mind with the sheer clamour of its desires. She was mindlessly, gloriously carried along on a tidal wave of physical pleasure.

What might have happened next, she never discovered. As Robb eased her shirt up over her breasts, freeing them so that he could kiss them with mounting passion, they were interrupted by the insistent clamour of the telephone.

'Don't answer it,' she said, fighting a feeling of foreboding.

'Somebody could be in trouble. I'd better take it.'

He was right. In the mountains, the telephone was a lifeline. They couldn't ignore it. All the same, as she tidied her clothes, she wished he had thought to switch on his answering machine.

It had all happened too quickly. She was unprepared for both the power and magic of his lovemaking and the suddenness of its end. She felt bereft, as if she had been deserted forever instead of just for a moment.

She looked up expectantly as Robb came back. 'What is it?'

His answering look was bleak. 'It's your editor, calling from Canberra.'

Her editor? She had intended to call Derek as soon as she returned to Robb's cabin but had overlooked it. In the flurry of their return and the need to rest her injured ankle she had forgotten her obligations.

Robb's lovemaking hadn't helped either.

She shot him a guilty look, but he appeared distracted. Then she understood. She was at the crossroads. She could decide to write the story and throw his father to the wolves, or disappoint herself and her editor. Whatever she decided, she was the loser.

She picked up the receiver. 'Hello, Derek.'

'Don't hello me. Where the hell have you been all this time?'

'I've been combing the mountains for a plane-wreck,' she reminded him. 'There's a shortage of public telephones in the wilderness.'

'Very funny. But then it isn't the first time one of my staff has disappeared in search of a story. The main thing is—did you find it?'

Indecision gripped her. 'I'm not sure.'

'Either you found the plane or you didn't,' he said with exaggerated patience.

'It's not that simple, Derek. There's something I didn't tell you before I took this assignment. It could complicate matters.' She took a deep breath, aware that Robb was listening intently to every word. 'I'm Jack Duncan's daughter.'

'Surprise me,' her editor sneered.

'You mean you already know?'

'Kenneth Shelton told me. He thought you might need some help on this story, someone more objective. I'm beginning to think he's right.'

'This is nothing to do with Kenneth,' she said carefully, conscious of Robb's sudden interest. 'I don't need him.'

'That's too bad, because he's on his way down there. When you didn't call, I told him to follow it up.'

'I presume he'll be reporting in regularly?' she asked.

'Unlike some journalists, Shelton does have a sense of responsibility.'

She ignored the jibe. 'Well, when he calls in, please tell him he's wasting his time coming down here.'

There was a disappointed silence. 'You mean you didn't find the plane after all?'

She hesitated. She had no intention of telling Derek everything, because in a split-second decision she knew what she had to do. But she baulked at telling an outright lie. 'We found the plane,' she said heavily. 'But ...'

'That's great, fantastic, all is forgiven,' enthused Derek from the other end of the line.

She paid little heed to his congratulations. She was too shaken by the discovery that Robb had waited only long enough to hear her last remark before storming out of the room.

Ignoring the editor's barrage of questions, she covered the mouthpiece with her hand. 'Robb, wait!'

But there was no answer. Moments later she heard a horse whinny, followed by the clatter of hooves which told her Robb was gone.

CHAPTER ELEVEN

GEMMA told herself she should be used to Robb's disappearing act by now, but as the hours passed and he didn't reappear she became alarmed.

If only he had waited to hear the rest of her conversation with her editor, he would have known where her loyalties lay.

Derek had been furious when she told him she wasn't going to write the story. But he contained his anger in order to reason with her.

'Being Jack Duncan's daughter makes it all the more important for you to set the record straight. You know everyone believed your father took off with the relief money. Now you can tell them the truth from his side.'

Kenneth had made sure that Derek knew all the details, she thought. 'There is no side to give. My father was innocent all along. We found the money intact. He lost his memory in the crash and didn't even know who he was until we told him.'

'Who is this "we"?' Derek asked keenly.

Damn! She hadn't meant to mention Robb's role in the search. In fact, she hadn't meant to discuss the story at all until Derek led her into it. His years as a television interviewer hadn't been wasted apparently. Reluctantly, she confessed, knowing he would press her until she did. 'My guide was a local man, Robb Wetherill.'

She could almost hear the wheels turning in Derek's head. 'The ski champion—son of the man who conducted the original search? My God, Gemma, you must write this story.'

There was no 'must' about it, she told herself, deciding to end this before it got out of hand. 'I'll let you know what I decide.'

Derek's protests were still spluttering down the line as she hung up the phone.

She looked around in indecision. With her ankle still troublesome, she couldn't think of leaving, although her car stood outside, mended and even freshly polished.

Since there was still no sign of Robb, she hobbled into the bathroom and washed her hair. She took a long time, applying masses of conditioner to make up for the effects of a week of neglect, letting the mindless activity calm her.

By the time she had finished it was almost sundown and she threw herself on to the couch in disgust. Why wouldn't Robb come back so that she could tell him that she wasn't going to write the story after all?

She had finally faced the fact that he meant more to her than all the Walkley awards in journalism. Even the need to clear her father's name was no longer so urgent now she knew the truth. Anyone who mattered would soon know it in any case, as soon as she and Robb returned the money.

So that left only her and Robb.

He had said he cared about her and his lovemaking seemed to confirm it. There was no denying the fire in his kisses or the need for her revealed in his embraces. He wanted her as much as she wanted him.

But would it be enough? She remembered her plan. If she went ahead with it, she would at least be near Robb, even if he never came to feel the same way about her as she did about him.

She debated whether to tell Robb what she had in mind, then decided to wait a while. If it didn't work, she would have no one to blame but herself.

It would work. It *had* to. The prospect of returning to a life without Robb was unthinkable. He had been gone only a short time and already she missed him unbearably.

More than anything, she missed his strong arms around her and his passionate mouth on hers, demanding a response she was only too willing to give. Just thinking about it made her skin feel hot in all the places he had touched her, and she stirred restlessly on the couch. Why didn't he come back?

As if in response to her prayer, there was a sound of a car pulling up outside. She hobbled to the window. Maybe someone had given Robb a lift back.

There were two men standing in the courtyard and her spirits plummeted. One of them was Kenneth Shelton. Whatever he said to Robb made him extremely angry. He shook his head and strode away in the direction of the paddock.

With a shrug, Kenneth walked towards the house. She was at the front door when he reached it, but there was no welcoming smile on her lips. 'What are you doing here?'

Kenneth smiled wryly. 'What a welcome for your fiancé.'

Her eyes darted past him, seeking another tall, broad-shouldered figure, but there was no sign of Robb. He must be with the horses. Reluctantly, she drew her eyes to Kenneth.

He seemed shorter and stockier since she had last seen him, but it could be in contrast to the man who had been in her thoughts all afternoon. Kenneth also had a hunted look, as if he were under pressure. Of course, any pressure he was under was usually of his own making. 'Ex-fiancé,' she said automatically.

He frowned. 'Breaking our engagement was your decision, not mine.'

'It wasn't a formal engagement, and you were quite happy with my decision,' she said tiredly. 'But it doesn't explain what you're doing here now.'

He looked uncomfortable. 'Couldn't we discuss this inside?'

Grudgingly, she stood aside to let him enter the living-room. He looked around with interest, his eye travelling to the bandage on her ankle, but he didn't comment on it. 'Derek thought I should help you cover the *Plains Drifter* story,' he began.

Her mouth tightened. 'I've already told him there's no story.' Derek must have sent Kenneth down here long before he telephoned her, so swift was his arrival.

'But you said you found the plane.'

So they had been in touch after all. 'Yes, we found it. But I decided to let sleeping dogs lie. The money will be returned to its owners and the location of the plane will stay a secret.'

'So your friend Wetherill insisted,' Kenneth grumbled. 'Derek thought he might be willing to talk if we made the offer large enough.'

They didn't know Robb as well as she did, or they wouldn't have wasted their time. 'What did Robb say?' she asked.

'I wouldn't repeat the words in front of a lady.'

She hid her relief. 'I'm glad you think I'm a lady. You didn't, last time we talked.'

'That was different. Finding the plane and the money removes the shadow over your past. There's no reason why we can't go on as before.' He regarded her hopefully.

She almost laughed aloud. Now that her father was exonerated and her slate was clean, Kenneth regretted his hasty decision. She would make a presentable wife for him after all for his political career. She would probably be even more of an asset because she had solved the mystery surrounding her father's disapperance. She could almost see the headlines now.

But she shook her head. 'It's too late for us, Kenneth. We were right to call it off. I don't love you.'

'So it's Wetherill, is it?'

His perceptiveness startled her. Were her feelings so transparent? 'Yes, I'm in love with Robb,' she confessed, surprising even herself. Now that she had said it aloud, she realised she had known it for a long time. She just hadn't admitted it to herself.

Ever the apprentice politician, Kenneth became gracious in defeat. 'In that case, I hope you two are happy together. But I warn you I'm not giving up on the story. There must be other guides around here who can help me track down the wreck.'

'Go ahead.' She could also afford to be generous, knowing how slim his chances were. But for her tumble down the hillside, she and Robb would have passed the place by.

Kenneth left soon afterwards, probably to try to recruit another guide. She was listlessly folding her clothes into her suitcase when Robb came back inside.

'Has Shelton left?'

'Yes. He didn't stay long. He went to town to try to hire another guide to take him to the wreck.'

There was a long-drawn silence. 'I see. So you're going with him as soon as you can find someone to take you there.'

She whirled on him, forgetting her injured ankle which gave way under her, so she sat down heavily on the bed. 'No! I said *he's* going to hire someone. I didn't say I was going with him.'

He looked at the open suitcase. 'But you're packing. Aren't you leaving with Shelton? He told me he had come to take you back with him.'

'He might have wanted to, but it doesn't mean I'm going.' Robb could be very obtuse when he chose. 'I don't want to go back to Canberra in any case.'

'But you're still going to write the story? I just came back from seeing my father in town and he's devastated by the news, but prepared for the worst. He says it's only justice after the way he treated your family.'

Taking his hand, she curled her fingers into his palm. 'Then you can tell him he needn't worry. His secret is safe with me.'

'But I heard you tell your editor about finding the plane,' he said, baffled.

'He asked me outright whether we had, and I couldn't lie to him. But if you hadn't rushed away you would have heard me refuse to reveal the location. Too many people's lives are involved to risk it—now or ever.'

Robb's rangy, six-foot-one frame had been hunched over. Now he sat upright, regarding her with astonishment. He raked a hand through his hair, rumpling it. 'Are you happy with your decision?'

Giving in to an urge which had bothered her for ages, she smoothed his hair down again, although a few strands curled around his ears and refused to be smoothed. She twined one such curl around her finger. 'If I weren't happy with my decision, I wouldn't have made it.'

His gold-flecked eyes devoured her. 'No, you wouldn't. You're a stubborn woman when you make up your mind. I should know. How many women would take off into the wilderness alone, as you did?'

'It was a crazy thing to do,' she acknowledged, 'but it achieved its purpose. You did follow me.'

'How could I do anything else? I was terrified some harm would come to you before I could persuade you to turn back.'

'But you failed, didn't you?' she teased. 'Even stealing all my supplies couldn't make me give up.'

'I have a feeling nothing would make you give up once you get an idea in your head.'

How right he was! But he couldn't know what sort of idea was in her head right now, or how far she was prepared to go to achieve her ends this time. 'Will you drive me to Omeo?' she asked.

'Omeo? But you said you turned down Shelton's offer of a lift back to Canberra.'

'Mainly because I'm not going to Canberra,' she said, savouring the coming dénouement as a child might relish the unwrapping of a parcel, layer by layer.

'So where are you going?' he asked, frustration making him irritable.

She lifted his hand and kissed the fingertips with great concentration. 'Nowhere. I'm staying in the High Plains. I'm probably out of a job after today and there's nothing else to take me back to Canberra. Now that Tony has his own career, he doesn't need me, and my aunt and uncle won't be sorry to see the last of their black sheep.'

'But what about your job?' You said you loved journalism, and this is hardly Fleet Street.'

'True, but I can write anywhere. Look at Joe McCabe. He writes his bush poetry from a little cabin in the mountains with no amenities. Bestsellers have been written in worse conditions. Or I'll get a job in the ski resorts, waitressing or something. I don't really care as long as it keeps me here. I'd like to be near Dad in case he ever regains his memory.'

'You're really prepared to give up everything to stay in the High Plains?'

'That's what I said.' What she didn't add was the real reason she had decided to stay. She wanted to prove to him that all city girls weren't alike. In time, he would learn to trust her enough to admit his feelings, as she now admitted hers. In time, he might even come to love her.

Robb began to pace restlessly around the small bedroom, dwarfing it with his breadth and height. He was wearing his favourite cartridge vest over a checked shirt, and he hooked his fingers into the empty cartridge pockets. 'But what about Kenneth Shelton? He must love you to trek all the way up here after you.'

'Kenneth hates to lose anything,' she said heavily. 'He's intensely competitive, which is one of the problems between us. If he hadn't been so ambitious about going into politics, he wouldn't have cared whether my father was innocent or guilty, only whether he loved me. It was only after he found out that I had erased the so-called shadow over my past that he decided he'd made a mistake. I would make a good politician's wife after all. But it was too late. I don't love Kennth, if I ever did.'

'You don't seem upset about it,' he observed.

She shrugged. 'Why should I? Everything I want is right here in the High Plains.'

His eyes lightened with a strangely hopeful glint, but he contained himself, saying levelly, 'You mean your father, I suppose.'

'Guess again.'

There was only one other possibility, and it struck him with the force of a thunderbolt. His eyes danced and his mouth quirked upwards into the beginnings of a grin, before he said tersely, 'My God, Gemma, don't joke about something like this. If you mean me, say so.'

Going to him, she rested her head against his deep chest, revelling in the earthy smells of leather and eucalyptus where he had brushed against the trees outside. There was also a faint but pleasant horsy scent which conjured up visions of riding alongside him up the steep slopes of Mount Hotham. 'Of course I mean you,' she breathed. 'I know now that you're the most important person in my life.'

His arms tightened around her and he kissed the top of her head, letting his lips linger there. 'I thought I'd never hear you admit it.' There was an edge of pain in his voice. 'I thought I was the only one who felt it.'

She twisted her head so that she could meet his eyes. 'Then you do care?'

'Care? Good lord, Gemma, don't you know by now how much I love you?'

Her heart soared. It was more than she had dared hope

to hear in so short a time. She had been prepared to wait as long as necessary for him to share her feelings. Now he was handing her his heart. She accepted the gift with due reverence. 'I love you, too. But I didn't dare hope you felt the same.'

'My fear exactly,' he confessed. 'When you seemed so determined to write that story, I was sure it meant more to you than I ever could.'

'Never that. When Derek called me today I realised that by hurting your father, I would be hurting you. And I couldn't do that for the world.'

He cleared his throat gruffly. 'You don't know how happy you've just made me, Gemma.'

'Because I'm not going to write the story?'

'No, because I know you love me. Nothing else matters. You know, I was almost going to ask you to stay here.'

'Then why didn't you?'

'I remembered the other times, when the attractions of the city won over anything I had to offer.'

'You didn't know I had already made my choice.' She linked her arms around his neck. 'I know what's good for me, Robb Wetherill.'

'Are you sure?' he asked huskily. 'You're giving up your whole way of life for me. It's a lot to ask.'

At his choice of words, her pulses raced. 'What exactly are you asking me?'

'I thought you understood. I love you and I want you to be my wife.'

She pouted prettily. 'This isn't at all the way I planned it.'

'How do you mean?'

'Well, first I was going to get a job locally. Then I

planned to get in your way often enough to convince you I was here to stay. *Then* you were supposed to propose.'

'Isn't this a lot quicker? Think of all the trouble I've saved you.'

'You've saved yourself, you mean,' she grinned cheekily. 'You've no idea what a nuisance I can be when I make up my mind to do something.'

'I have a pretty good idea.' She knew he was thinking of how she had lured him up the mountain after her. 'So I'd better stop you being a nuisance and marry you.'

'In that case, I accept, with all my heart.'

He captured her mouth in a long, lingering kiss which set the blood singing in her veins. Ardently she responded, putting into her pliant lips all the love she felt for her indomitable mountain man.

She could hardly believe it had come to this. From being prepared to wait as long as it took to have him by her side she had made the giant leap to accepting his proposal of marriage. She giggled into his chest.

He tilted her chin she that she was looking up at him. 'What's so funny?'

'I was thinking—with a courtship conducted at this speed, what will our marriage be like?'

'A breathless affair, I should think,' he agreed gravely, then joined his laughter to hers.

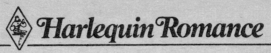 *Harlequin Romance*

Coming Next Month

Available in October wherever paperback books are sold, or through Harlequin Reader Service:

In the U.S.
901 Fuhrmann Blvd.
P.O. Box 1397
Buffalo, N.Y. 14240-1397

In Canada
P.O. Box 603
Fort Erie, Ontario
L2A 5X3

Temptation ™

TEMPTATION WILL BE
EVEN HARDER TO RESIST...

In September, Temptation is presenting a sophisticated new face to the world. A fresh look that truly brings Harlequin's most intimate romances into focus.

What's more, all-time favorite authors Barbara Delinsky, Rita Clay Estrada, Jayne Ann Krentz and Vicki Lewis Thompson will join forces to help us celebrate. The result? A very special quartet of Temptations...

- **Four striking covers**
- **Four stellar authors**
- **Four sensual love stories**
- **Four variations on one spellbinding theme**

All in one great month! Give in to Temptation in September.

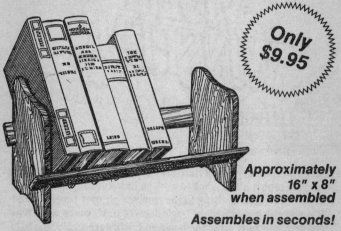

HARLEQUIN SIGNATURE EDITION

VIOLET WINSPEAR

HOUSE OF STORMS

Editorial secretary Debra Hartway travels to the Salvador family's rugged Cornish island home to work on Jack Salvador's latest book. Disturbing questions hang in the troubled air over Lovelis Island. What or who had caused the tragic death of Jack's young wife? Why did Jack stay away from the home and, more especially, the baby son he loved so well? And—why should Rodare, Jack's brother, who had proved himself a man of the highest integrity, constantly invade Debra's thoughts with such passionate, dark desires . . .?

Violet Winspear, who has written more than 65 romance novels translated worldwide into 18 languages, is one of Harlequin's best-loved and bestselling authors. HOUSE OF STORMS, her second title in the Harlequin Signature Edition program, is a full-length novel rich in romantic tradition and intriguingly spiced with an atmosphere of danger and mystery.

Watch for HOUSE OF STORMS—coming in October!

HOFS-1